ABOUT THIS BOOK

CHRISTMAS WITH IDA EARLY
by Robert Burch

Zany and fun-loving Ida Early returns, in this high-spirited sequel
to *Ida Early Comes Over the Mountain*. When a new preacher comes to
town, she goes along with his plans for a solemn reenactment of
the Christmas story. But Ida—with her knack for show business—
makes it a decidedly unconventional celebration.

Ida's antics and adventures serve as examples of humor in all its
guises—raucous, whimsical, poignant, and witty. From barnyard
ventriloquism to a chaotic Christmas tableau, Ida Early's tall tales
become reality, in a captivating story that will delight her many fans.

Christmas With Ida Early

Christmas
With
Ida Early

Robert Burch

SCHOLASTIC INC.
New York Toronto London Auckland Sydney

Cover illustration by Richard Williams.

ISBN 0-590-43951-0

12 11 10 9 8 7 6 5 4 3 2 1   0 1 2 3 4 5/9

Printed in the U.S.A.   40
First Scholastic printing, November 1990

For Pete Jones
and
Susan Jones

Contents

Contents

Christmas With Ida Early

The Thanksgiving Turkey

Ida Early was so tall that she used the top of the Suttons' big icebox as a kitchen counter. She pushed the wire egg basket to one side and began breaking eggs over a mixing bowl. After each white fell into the bowl, she raised the shell, took aim, and tossed the yolk into a boiler on the stove halfway across the room.

"Want me to stir?" asked Randall, getting up from the table where he and Ellen had been studying. "I've finished my homework."

"That might speed things along," said Ida. "Just sort of mix the yellows into that sugar mixture." She was making boiled custard, a favorite of all the Suttons. "We need about six more. Are you ready?"

"Ready on the right!" said Randall, moving his hand and the spoon out of the way just as an egg yolk landed in the boiler.

"Bull's-eye!" he shouted, and after he'd stirred for a moment, Ida called, "Ready?"

"Ready on the left!" he said, and another yolk hit the mixture. When he'd gone through, "Ready on the right," "Ready on the left," and, "Ready on the firing line," twice, he said, "That's it; that's six."

"And one for good measure," said Ida. "Stand back."

Randall stood back from the boiler, and Ida broke one more egg. After the white had fallen away, she said, "Behold! A hook shot," and tossed the yolk so high that it almost hit the ceiling. Then *splat*, it dropped neatly into the boiler.

A few minutes later Ida took over the stirring. Randall watched as she added rich cream and milk to the custard. "Where are the twins?" he asked.

"They're outside being kind to the turkey," said Ida, adjusting a strap of her overalls. Randall was glad that she'd gone back to wearing them. She'd worn nothing but overalls when she first came, and they somehow seemed right for her. Still, Randall had thought the day she arrived that she looked like a cross between a scarecrow and a telephone pole. He guessed that was because he'd never seen a grown woman wearing overalls and men's shoes. Also, he'd never seen a woman—or a man—quite so tall. Ida insisted that she wasn't especially tall, that she was as near six feet as she was seven, but her height definitely made her different from most folks in the mountains of northern Georgia. The July day she'd arrived she'd been a bit windblown, too, but later, when she'd freshened up and brushed her hair, she'd looked nice enough. By now Randall considered her as pretty—in a breezy, healthy sort of way—as any other young woman. And she was young—"Nearer twenty than thirty," she put it.

"The turkey is to be our Thanskgiving dinner," said Randall.

"Yes, I know," said Ida. "That's why the twins are out being kind to it. They want it to be happy today because tomorrow it's gonna have its head chopped off."

"They make pets out of everything," said Randall, shaking his head. Of course, when he'd been six he'd done the same thing. Still, the turkey had been here less than a week, and the twins had known from the start why it had been bought.

Ellen, at the big table in the center of the room, closed her notebook. "Finished!" she said triumphantly. She was in the seventh grade this year and Randall in the sixth. They tried to do their schoolwork in the afternoon so that in the evening they could have fun with the rest of the family. Whenever Mr. Sutton wasn't too tired from his work at the lumberyard in Buckley, he'd play a card game with them—or board games like checkers and tiddlywinks. Or they'd listen to radio programs together, or someone might read aloud from the big *Hearthside Book of Stories*. Also, Ida would sometimes tell about adventures she'd had—or adventures she'd made up but pretended to have had.

Mrs. Sutton had died in the spring, and Ida Early looked after the house and the family now. Before she'd arrived, cross old Aunt Earnestine had come to the mountains to look after them. It was a happy occasion when Ida Early came along and Aunt Earnestine went home to Atlanta. Ida had gone away for a while recently, but she was back now and everybody was happy. Randall hoped she wouldn't go away again.

Ellen stood up and stretched. "Being kind to the turkey must mean tying a string around its neck and leading it around the yard. That's what they were doing earlier." She walked over to the window. "Nope! They've thrown the string away now, and the turkey's following them on its own."

Ida and Randall joined her at the window, and all of them laughed when they saw Clay, Dewey, and the turkey running around the yard as if they were playing follow-the-leader. Two guineas, the red rooster, and a duck—pets of the twins—peeked out from behind the woodpile, puzzled by this strange game.

Clay was the leader. He took a few steps, and Dewey ran after him. Then the turkey ran to catch up with them. When Clay slowed down, Dewey and the turkey slowed down. When they came to the big tree stump that was used as a chopping block, Clay hopped on the stump, waved his arms, and hopped down. The turkey flew over the stump.

"I don't blame it," said Ida. "If I were a turkey two days before Thanksgiving, I wouldn't perch on a chopping block either." Then she said, "It's too bad to break up the fun, but the boys should have a bath."

Randall went to the yard and told the twins that Ida wanted them inside. He didn't tell them they were to bathe; he'd let Ida handle that. The mention of soap and water always brought on arguments from the twins.

Randall went back into the kitchen with Clay and Dewey. The room was called the kitchen, but it served as dining room and family sitting room as well. Bedrooms were off the front hall, and there was a parlor, which was called the front room. But the parlor was seldom used; the family did most of its living in the big kitchen.

"We want the turkey to come inside, too," said Clay.

"You can keep an eye on it from in here," said Ida. She reached out and clasped both of them by their shoulders, then added, "While you have a bath. Your pa may bring the new preacher home for supper, and you'll want to be all shined up to meet him. Now won't you?"

Clay and Dewy tried to run away. Although they were wiry and small for their age, they were also strong, but Ida held on to them. Soon both of them were in the washtub that was on the floor near the stove. They could both fit into it at the same time, with splashing space left over. As always, they laughed and yelled and appeared to be having such a good time that Randall wondered why they always fought the idea of taking a bath.

After a few moments Dewey said, "You said we could watch the turkey from here."

"So I did," said Ida. She went over to the door and

propped it open. The afternoon sunshine came into the room; it seemed more like spring than late November. "See," said Ida, "the turkey's not missing you too much. It's struck up a friendship with Frizzy." Frizzy was a frizzled hen, also a pet. But the turkey, seeing the door open, left the chicken and walked up the steps and across the porch. It stood in the doorway to the kitchen and looked around.

"Let's give it a bath," said Clay.

"No," said Ida.

"Why?"

"Because turkeys don't like to bathe."

"We don't like to bathe either," said Clay, starting out of the tub. Ida reached across and sat him down in the water.

The twins went back to splashing, and Randall, sitting in his father's big chair near the fireplace, was reading *Li'l Abner* on the comic page of the day's newspaper when suddenly there was a *swoosh*. The turkey had flown into the room. It landed on the top rung of a straight chair. For a few seconds the chair tilted backward slightly—then it leaned out farther . . . and farther. Just as it crashed to the floor, the turkey flapped its wings and flew into the air. It circled the room once and, on its second time around, lit on a tall cupboard in the corner. Almost at the ceiling, the turkey nestled onto the top shelf that looked as if it had been put there for a roost, and gobbled contentedly.

"Very well," said Ida, "you can perch up there. But you've got to get out of here by suppertime."

The turkey gobbled again, and Ida, pretending to be upset, asked, "What do you mean, you might or you might not? Don't be a smart aleck, or I'll quit teaching you to talk!"

"Can you really teach animals to talk?" asked Dewey.

"Oh, sure! When I was a big star on a radio program, I had lots of talking animals." Randall laughed. There weren't many things Ida didn't claim to have done. Sometimes she'd actually done them.

The turkey gobbled again. "Hear that gobbling noise it makes?" said Ida. "Well, it's just a matter of days before it'll be talking clear as anything."

Randall said, "It better learn in one day! That's all it's got left!"

Dewey said, "Maybe if it could talk, Pa wouldn't want to kill it for Thanksgiving. He'd let us have it for our circus." The twins and Ida were always saying they'd have a circus someday. They'd use Frizzy and their other pets—and a goat, which the twins wanted more than anything else in the world—and maybe a few trained dogs, which they'd buy and train after they'd bought and trained the goat.

Clay asked, "Do you think you can teach the turkey to talk in one day?"

"I'll try," said Ida. "If you'll scrub behind your ears now, and then put on your clean clothes, I'll surely try." The twins splashed a little water at the back of their necks and jumped out and ran toward their room without drying off.

Ida whirled a towel over her head and let it sail across the kitchen. It reached the doorway just as Clay and Dewey did and dropped over them like a tent.

Nobody was surprised. Ida had perfect aim.

The Guest

At almost dark, Mr. Sutton drove into the yard. Ida and the children stood at a window in the kitchen. The only person with Mr. Sutton looked to be a teenage boy. "We can relax," said Randall. "That's no preacher."

"Who is it then?" asked Ida, looking over his shoulder.

"Maybe somebody helping set up a new piece of equipment at the lumberyard," said Randall. The young man had on khaki work pants, a sweater, and what looked like a baseball cap. He and Mr. Sutton were starting toward the back door.

"And besides," said Ellen, "if it was a preacher, Pa'd bring him to the front door."

Mr. Sutton and his guest walked into the kitchen. "Come on in," said Mr. Sutton, "and meet everybody." He glanced around the room. "Looks like the gang's all here! Boys and girls, meet my new friend, Mr. Preston."

"Pleased to meet you," said Randall, stepping forward and shaking hands.

"Us too," said Clay. "We're pleased to meet you, too," and the twins shook hands with him and then with each other. They always shook hands with each other after greeting anyone else.

Ellen greeted the young man next, and then Ida took his hand and pumped it up and down. "We're all glad to meet you. Yes, indeed, it's our pleasure! Why, we were standing around here waiting to welcome a tired old man, and what shows up but a mere child! Life's full of surprises."

"Evidently I look young for my age. I'm past twenty."

Ida laughed. "So am I. But have off your cap and stay awhile. Any friend of Mr. Sutton's is a friend of ours."

"Well, thank you," said Mr. Preston. He took off his cap, and a strand of red hair fell onto his freckled forehead. He glanced at the hatrack in the corner and then flipped his cap across the room. It landed on a peg.

"We thought Ida was the only one who could do that," said Dewey.

Mr. Preston smiled. "You mean Ida's got a good throwing arm, too?"

"It's in the wrist movement," explained Clay. Ida was always saying the secret of her good aim was in the wrist movement. He looked up at Ida and said, "Tell him about the time you threw a rock at a dime that an old man pitched way up in the sky."

"I've heard of people shooting at coins to test their marksmanship," said their visitor. "I somehow can't imagine anyone throwing at a dime and being able to hit it."

"Ida could," said Clay. "She hit that one so hard it broke into a million pieces."

"Oh, come now!"

"You did, didn't you, Ida?" said Dewey. He and Clay were smiling proudly up at her.

"Well, no, not exactly," said Ida, and Mr. Preston said, "I thought not."

Clay's and Dewey's smiles disappeared. Ida looked down at their long faces and was quiet for a moment. Then she said, "No, of course, I didn't knock it into a *million* pieces." She tousled Dewey's hair. "I knocked it into *ten* pieces."

The twins smiled up at Ida again as she explained to their guest, "Ten pennies, to be exact. I wish you could have seen that ol' man's face while he stood there waiting for his dime to come back to the ground and all of a sudden pennies sprinkled down on him! That's how that song, 'Pennies from Heaven,' came about—maybe we'll sing it for you sometime. Do you like music?"

The visitor looked as if he wondered how he'd been led into this conversation.

Mr. Sutton, sitting down in a rocker over by the fireplace, motioned toward the big armchair where he usually sat. "Come on around and have a seat. Most likely we're gonna have some supper by and by."

"We're to have a good one," said Ellen, opening the door to the oven to check on biscuits that Ida had made.

Dewey stood on one side of their visitor and Clay on the other, looking up at him as if he were a skyscraper. Randall could guess sometimes what his younger brothers were thinking. For a moment he was afraid they were about to ask Mr. Preston to stand back to back with Ida so they could see which one was taller. Their visitor was tall, well over six feet, but not as tall as Ida. Few people were. Randall was relieved when Mr. Preston sat down and the twins took their places on each side of the hearth.

Ellen and Randall got busy clearing their books off the table and setting it for supper. Ida, turning chicken that was frying in an iron skillet, called across the room, "You're in luck, Mr. Preston! We were fixing a meal fit for a preacher."

Dewey said, "But we're glad you came instead."

"Yeah," said Clay. "But if we'd known it was you, we might not've had to take a bath."

Mr. Preston smiled. "Why's that?"

"We had to clean up because we thought a preacher might come for supper."

"But I *am* a preacher."

"What?" asked Ellen and Randall at the same time.

Ida came away from the stove and faced him. "You don't look like any preacher I ever saw."

"I can't help that. But for what it's worth, I just recently graduated from the seminary and was sent here to take your preacher's place."

"He wasn't my preacher," said Ida. "I'm just visiting here."

Clay and Dewey sprang up from the hearth as if somebody had shot at them—and looked just as alarmed. Before they could say anything, Ida said, "Okay! Okay! I live here."

Randall knew that all she'd meant was that she wasn't in the church, but still, the twins didn't want her considered a visitor instead of a member of the family. They settled back down, and Mr. Preston said, "I'm sorry if my looks disappoint you."

"Why, no," said Ida, "that's not what we meant."

"It's my fault," Mr. Sutton said. "I should have introduced you as our new minister, Brother Preston. But I thought the gang understood." Turning to Ida and the children, he added, "When I dropped by his house just now to see if he'd like to come eat with us, he was in the yard raking leaves. I insisted that he come the way he was."

Dewey looked up at the young minister and said, "We like your looks just fine."

"Yes," said Clay. "We think you look just fine, *Brother* Preston."

Mr. Sutton patted Clay on the head. "There," he said. "Now we've got it. And, Brother Preston, part of the mix-up, no doubt, was because we've been used to Brother Thaxton, and he was considerably older than you."

"Considerably more solemn, too," added Ellen. "We never saw him smile."

"I did," said Clay, always one to argue. "I saw him smile once upon a time."

"When was that?" asked Ellen.

"When Mamma died. He told Dewey and me that she was in heaven, and then he smiled, didn't he, Dewey?"

Randall thought about his mother. It wasn't until recently that anyone could speak of her that he didn't feel as if he might cry.

"He said she was in heaven," agreed Dewey. "I don't remember him smiling."

"Well, he did," insisted Clay. "I know he did."

"All right. All right," said Mr. Sutton, which meant they were not to argue about it. To Brother Preston he said, "Brother Thaxton was serious by nature, which is all right, but we're glad you know how to laugh."

"Oh, I think a sense of humor is important."

Ida announced that supper was ready, and everybody found a place at the table. "Let's bow our heads," said Mr. Sutton, "and, Brother Preston, why don't you return thanks?"

Brother Preston asked the blessing, which was much longer than Mr. Sutton's usual one. Mr. Sutton—and his children, whenever he asked one of them to say the blessing—had a memorized one that they always used: "Lord, make us thankful for these and all Thy many blessings. Amen." But Brother Preston turned the blessing into a long prayer, saying how glad he was to be with this fine family, who had made him feel so welcome—taking him into their home and hearts so openly on first meeting him. Also he prayed that God would watch over him in this, his first ministry. He went on and on.

Randall peeked at all the good food Ida had prepared that was getting cold. He remembered his father once saying that he believed there was a course taught at the seminary called "How to Be Long-winded." Finally Brother Preston brought the blessing to an end with, "And bless these Sutton children, dear Lord, and their father. Amen."

"What about Ida?" asked Clay, when everyone had looked up. Randall lifted the platter of fried chicken, offering it to Brother Preston.

"What do you mean, what about me?" asked Ida. "I'm right here. Now help yourself to some of those string beans and pass them along."

"No," said Clay, looking up at Brother Preston, who sat next to him. "I mean you didn't ask God to bless Ida. You asked him to bless us and Pa—and to look after you."

"That's right," said Dewey, taking a biscuit from

the bread plate that Ellen was holding. "You skipped over Ida." He put the biscuit back onto the plate and said, "We'd better do it again. Everybody, bow your heads."

Randall thought, Oh, no, we're not ever going to eat if he says another blessing. He expected his father to tell the twins to go ahead and serve their plates, that the blessing had been asked, but Brother Preston spoke first. "Of course, you're right. I should have remembered." He asked another blessing. This one was much shorter, and he included Ida in it as well as the children and Mr. Sutton.

During the meal Brother Preston told funny stories, stopping every now and then to load up his plate with chicken and all the other good dishes. Another course at the seminary, thought Randall: How to Eat More than Anybody Else. Ida had always said that she was complimented when anyone ate lots of her cooking, so she must be feeling fine just now.

One of Brother Preston's stories was about a summer job he'd had after his first year in college. He'd worked on a farm near the college, and his pay had been two goats. He couldn't afford to have them shipped home, so he'd hitchhiked the two hundred miles with them.

The twins were delighted to hear a story about

goats, and they wanted to know all about the ones that had hitchhiked across the state. "What happened to them after you got home?" asked Dewey.

"We kept them till I went back to college a few weeks later. Then my folks sold them to the local butcher."

Of course, the twins were disappointed that the story ended in such a way. Randall couldn't help thinking that if Ida Early were telling it, no matter what had really happened, it would have been different. Probably she'd have said that the goats had gone on to become something grand—the main attraction in an animal show, no doubt—and people had come from miles around just to see them.

There was a lull in the conversation until Dewey asked Brother Preston, "Are you married?"

"No, I'm not."

Clay asked, "Then would you like to get married?"

Brother Preston laughed. "Well, yes, sooner or later I suppose I would."

Mr. Sutton said, "I imagine most of you fellows in the ministry get married sooner instead of later. In rural charges especially, I'd think a minister's wife is almost a necessity. With everything from church suppers to choir practice, you'd need a helpmeet—or is it helpmate?"

"Either," said Brother Preston. "In the Bible, the second chapter of Genesis, there's mention of a helpmeet for Adam. In any case, I'll want to get married. Some other congregations wouldn't hire a man who didn't have a wife."

Ellen said, "You make it sound a bit like a business proposition." Randall was afraid that his father might consider this impertinent and scold Ellen, but when he looked across the table at him, Mr. Sutton winked at him.

Brother Preston, however, was not amused. He turned to Ellen. "No, I just meant . . . well . . ." and his face turned red. He sounded almost angry when he added, "Working for the Lord *is* a serious business."

"I see," said Ellen.

Everyone was quiet for a moment, and then Dewey said, "Maybe you'd like to marry Ida?"

Randall noticed that Ida blushed, and he wondered what she'd do. He should have known she'd laugh. "That's a good idea," she said. "Brother Preston, why don't you marry me? Thank you, Dewey, for thinking up such a splendid suggestion!"

"You're welcome," said Dewey in his soft voice.

Mr. Sutton asked, "But what'd happen to our family if Ida hauled off and got married and moved away from us?"

"We'd haul off and go with her," said Dewey. "You'd take us with you, wouldn't you, Ida?"

Ida reached across the table and put one hand on top of his. "I wouldn't budge a step without you," she said.

Thanksgiving Eve

At breakfast Mr. Sutton reminded Randall of jobs to be done after school. There was wood to be chopped and a place in the pasture fence to be mended. As if it were an afterthought, he added, "And kill the turkey."

"We don't want to kill the turkey," said Dewey.

"No, we don't!" shouted Clay.

"Now be calm," said their father. "I don't want *you* to kill it. That's a job for Randall."

Most of the time Randall was glad to be the oldest boy in the family. It was nice to have his father treat him as if he were almost grown. But there were times when it wasn't so good; being asked to kill the turkey was one of them.

Mr. Sutton tried to reason with Clay and Dewey. "It's a lesson we all have to learn. It may seem cruel to you, but it's a hard fact of country life that we can't always keep farm animals as pets." The twins didn't act as if they'd even heard him till he added, "And besides, we have enough freeloaders in the yard already."

"What are freeloaders?" asked Dewey.

"Somebody who eats free food but doesn't do anything in return."

"We don't have any freeloaders," said Clay.

"Yes, I'm afraid we do," said his father. "Besides your two guineas and the duck, there's the red rooster that we don't need but can't put in the pot because it's your pet. And what about the frizzled hen? She's never laid an egg in her life, but she can't be Sunday dinner for us because she's your pet."

"Frizzy's too tired to lay eggs," said Ellen. "The twins wear her out playing with her."

"She's a frazzled frizzled hen," said Randall, and Ellen giggled.

Mr. Sutton leaned over and patted Clay and Dewey on their shoulders. "So this afternoon Randall will do his job, and then Ida will dress the turkey."

"Dress it?" said Clay.

"Pluck it and clean it and get it ready to be cooked."

Ellen, pouring a glass of milk from the big pitcher, laughed. "Clay thought 'dress it' meant put clothes on it!"

"I did not!"

"Yes, you did," Ellen insisted. "You thought Ida would put shoes and socks on the turkey—and maybe a little pair of overalls."

Dewey looked up at Ida and said, "Guess what, Ida? If you put overalls on the turkey, it would look just like you."

Ida brushed a crumb off the bib of her overalls. "Why, Dewey, do you think I'm as ugly as a turkey?"

"Oh, no," said Dewey, sounding distressed that she would think such a thing. "I think you're *pretty* as a turkey!"

Clay added, "Turkeys are the prettiest things in the world."

Mr. Sutton laughed, and Ida, spreading strawberry jam onto biscuits for the twins, said, "In that case, if I were putting clothes on it, I think I'd try to find it a nice little pair of lounging pajamas."

"Lounging pajamas?" said Clay.

"They're the latest thing," said Ida, smiling

brightly. "Ladies wear 'em when they're lounging around."

"What's 'lounging around'?"

"Oh, you know," Ida said. "Lounging is sitting around shelling peas or reading the funny papers or playing checkers—things like that."

Ellen said, "When rich ladies lounge around, they sit on sofas with satin pillows everywhere and a little dog in their lap and a big box of candy off to one side."

Mr. Sutton laughed. "How'd you come to know about rich ladies, Ellen?"

"I saw a picture in a magazine at school."

Ida pointed to the clock on the mantelpiece. "It's *that time!*" she said, and the children hopped up from the table. Ellen grabbed her books, took Dewey by one hand, and hurried out of the house. Randall took his books and Clay; the bus got to the stop just as they did. The twins didn't like school, and when left on their own they often missed the bus. Today's mad dash had become the routine.

During the day Randall kept thinking about the Thanksgiving holidays that were about to begin. Somehow he wasn't happy about them. Maybe this was partly because Aunt Earnestine was coming. No doubt, she'd complain about everything the children did. Another reason he couldn't get excited about Thanksgiving was the task he'd been assigned; he dreaded killing the turkey. If only the twins wouldn't take it so hard. He'd seen them across the playground at recess, and instead of joining the other children in their games, they'd stood off by themselves. And on the bus ride home neither looked as if he'd ever laughed in his life.

At home Randall read the comics in the day's paper, spending more time on them than usual. Then he set about his regular chores, drawing them out as long as he could. In late afternoon he knew he'd put off killing the turkey as long as possible, and he went out to the henhouse to get it. Sure enough, Clay and Dewey were there, patting the turkey as if it were an old, old pal. The turkey made a contented gobbling noise as if he considered them special, too.

Although the twins might not understand, they didn't cry over anything they couldn't help. So when Randall picked up the turkey and started toward the woodpile, they followed silently—like mourners in a funeral procession.

Ida Early was sitting in the late afternoon sunshine, peeling potatoes. She sat on an old nail keg, leaning against the side of the toolshed. The pan was in her lap. Often she brought work into the yard when the weather was pleasant, but usually she sat on the back steps.

After arranging the turkey so that its neck stretched over the chopping block, Randall reached for the ax. The twins stood back, looking first at him and then at the turkey. He wished they'd scream at him—shout, "Don't do it!" or something. But they stood motionless and silent.

For a moment Randall did not move either. Then he put down the ax. "I can't do it," he said, as much to himself as to anyone else. He sat down on the block, the turkey across his lap, and pounded his forehead with the palm of his hand.

Nobody said a word until a car drove into the yard a few moments later. "It's Pa," said Randall.

"Why's he home?" asked Dewey, but before anyone could answer, Mr. Sutton had walked out to the woodpile. "What's happening out here?" he asked cheerfully. "Why are we all gathered together?"

"We're not *all* gathered together," said Clay. "Ellen's in the house."

Mr. Sutton swung Clay into the air and then hugged him. He did the same for Dewey. "Well, almost all. Is it a Thanksgiving Eve party? And am I invited? We closed the lumberyard early so that everybody could go home and start being thankful."

It was then that he saw the turkey. "What?" he said "It's not in the icebox yet? That was one of the things I expected to be thankful for—that tomorrow's dinner was nearly ready."

Randall stood up. "I couldn't do it," he said, holding out the turkey. He and his father looked at each other. He half expected to hear a lecture on the hard facts of country life, but his father reached out and took the turkey. "It's all right. I'll do it."

Mr. Sutton stretched the turkey's neck across the block and picked up the ax. Just as he was taking aim, the turkey said, "Oh, please don't!" It shocked Randall, who was standing beside his father, and he jumped back.

"What's the matter?" asked Ida, looking up from her work.

"Nothing," said Randall. "It's just that for a minute I thought—" Suddenly he felt silly. Of course, he knew a turkey couldn't talk. His concern about killing it must have affected his mind; it was playing tricks on him. At the same time, he realized that his father must've heard something, too, because he'd let the turkey go.

The turkey, now that it was free, did not run away. It stepped gingerly around the top of the chopping block.

"Look, Ida!" said Dewey. "The turkey's dancing!"

"Of course it is," said Ida. "If somebody had been about to chop your head off and suddenly turned you loose, wouldn't you do a step or two?"

Then the turkey stretched its wings and fanned out its tail. "Why, look at that turkey strut!" said Ida. "We shouldn't eat a turkey who can do that."

Mr. Sutton said, "Any turkey tom can strut."

"No, that one's special," Ida insisted. "It should become a circus turkey."

"We'll use it in our animal act," said Dewey.

"No!" said Mr. Sutton emphatically. "It was bought for Thanksgiving." He grabbed the turkey and in a flash had the ax poised a second time, the turkey's neck stretched over the block.

"I do wish you wouldn't!" said the turkey, louder this time, and Mr. Sutton put down the ax. He looked around. "Something's going on around here!" he said. "Or else I'm hearing voices."

"I didn't hear any voices," said Clay.

"Me either," said Dewey.

"All I heard was the turkey talking," said Clay, as if it had been the most natural thing in the world.

"That's all I heard, too," said Dewey. "It said, 'I do wish you wouldn't!' "

"Yes," said Clay, "that's what I heard it say, too. It

meant he wished nobody would kill it."

"We know what it meant!" snapped Randall.

Ida said, "Now if that turkey can talk, we certainly ought not to cook it."

Mr. Sutton asked, "Will we have anything to eat tomorrow if I spare it? I've invited Brother Preston to eat with us again."

"Oh, I've got all sorts of good things cooked," said Ida. "I've been in the kitchen all day."

Then the turkey said—or at least it sounded as if the turkey were saying it—"Don't look so sad, Randall. Everything'll be all right." Before it had finished, Randall looked at Ida, who had her head bent down, pretending to have gone back to peeling potatoes. But he saw that her lips were moving. Why, that was it—she was throwing her voice. She was a ventriloquist, that's what she was. Like the man who'd put on a program at school last year; he'd sat on the stage with a wooden doll in his lap and made it appear that the doll was talking. And like Edgar Bergen on the radio; he and his dummies, Charlie McCarthy and Mortimer Snerd, were Sunday night favorites of the Sutton family. Charlie was always so clever, and Mortimer was such a dumb country bumpkin.

Randall looked at his father, who was smiling.

Then Randall looked at Ida. "You wouldn't be like Edgar Bergen, would you?"

"Who, me?" said Ida. "Of course not!" She sounded surprised that he would ask such a thing.

Then the turkey said, "She's more like Mortimer Snerd!"

Mr. Sutton and Randall laughed, but the twins became angry. "She's not so!" said Clay, talking to the turkey. "Mortimer Snerd is dumb, and Ida's not dumb!"

"No, she's not!" echoed Dewey.

The turkey said, "I was only teasing."

The twins had not caught on to who was doing the talking. Even if they had, Randall knew they'd take it as just something else that Ida could do that was magic and wonderful.

Aunt Earnestine Returns

Randall was at the roadside on Thanksgiving morning, gathering pecans that had fallen beneath the tree near the mailbox, when his father returned home with Aunt Earnestine. Although it was a holiday, Mr. Sutton had had to go to the lumberyard to check on the machinery. He'd timed the trip so that he could meet Aunt Earnestine, who'd come by bus from Atlanta.

After Mrs. Sutton died, Aunt Earnestine had looked after the Sutton household. Randall supposed it had been generous of her to give up her life in Atlanta to come and look after them, but she'd been so bossy and strict that he'd been glad when she went home. This time she was coming for Thanksgiving weekend. That was long enough.

Instead of going into the backyard where he usually parked, Mr. Sutton pulled up to the front walk. "Give your aunt a hand with her suitcase," he called to Randall. "I have to go back and work awhile longer."

Randall hurried to the car and, after greeting Aunt Earnestine, reached into the back seat for the suitcase. "Handle it carefully," she said.

Randall asked his father, "Don't you want to wait and eat? It'll soon be time for lunch."

"I know, but there's a problem with a thermostat on one of the kilns. But I'll be back by night for our Thanksgiving feast. Don't start it without me!"

"We won't," called Randall as his father drove away.

"Careful that the clasps don't come undone," said Aunt Earnestine as she and Randall started up the walk. When he shifted the suitcase from one hand to the other, she scolded, "Now watch what you're doing! Don't drop it!" That was like her, he thought. A simple task like taking a suitcase into the house didn't need so much comment. Couldn't she say something like, "Tell me how things are going with you, Randall," or maybe ask, "How's school this year?" It came to him that he could say something pleasant himself, so he said, "How are things going with you, Aunt Earnestine?"

It took her by surprise. "Oh, all right," she said. Then she added, "Now don't hit that top step." He'd never been able to figure out how anyone so unpleasant could be his father's sister.

Ellen came out the front door onto the porch. She was holding the door open for them, but she let it slam shut when Aunt Earnestine screamed, "Ellen!" as if she'd been stricken by sudden pain.

"Yes, ma'am?" said Ellen. "What's the matter?"

"That dress! It's much too short."

Ellen had made the dress last year in a sewing class, and usually when she wore it she received two compliments: one because the dress was pretty and the other because she'd made it herself. Of course, she had grown quite a bit this past year—"shot up," her father said—and maybe she was outgrowing the dress.

Aunt Earnestine added, "And it's a summer weight and color."

Ellen looked hurt but didn't say anything. Randall said, "But we've been having a warm spell. It's almost like summer."

"Yes, dear, I know," said Aunt Earnestine. "And she made the dress in home economics. But she needs someone here to tell her what's appropriate to wear."

It was criticism aimed directly at Ida Early, Randall knew. And it had been said loudly—so that anyone in the house could hear. Aunt Earnestine had never approved of Ida. She and Aunt Myrtle had tried to persuade Mr. Sutton to find someone else to look after his family.

Ida came into the front hallway. "Well, howdy-do?" she said cheerily. If she'd heard what had been said, she didn't seem bothered by it.

Aunt Earnestine said coolly, "Hello."

"Come on back to the kitchen," said Ida, "and have off your things and tell us what's happening nowadays in the city."

"Nothing's happening," said Aunt Earnestine. "Nothing of interest."

Ida said, "Randall, just throw the suitcase in my room." She explained to Aunt Earnestine, "I'm moving in with Ellen for the next few days."

"Don't *throw* it anywhere," said Aunt Earnestine.

"I'll be careful," said Randall, putting the suitcase just inside the bedroom door.

In the kitchen Aunt Earnestine took off her jacket

and held it out to Ida. "You may take this," she said. Randall and Ellen looked at each other. He knew she was thinking the same thing he was: Ida should be treated like a member of the family, not like a servant.

"Take it where?" asked Ida, grinning.

"Just hang it up."

Ida took the jacket, and Randall thought, Here it comes! One of Ida's specialties was throwing things, including clothes, and making them land wherever she chose. She said it saved steps in doing the housework; Aunt Earnestine should have remembered. But Ida surprised him. She took the jacket across the room and hung it neatly on the hatrack.

Aunt Earnestine sniffed. Randall couldn't tell if she was relieved or disappointed. Maybe she wanted Ida to do things that she considered improper; it would give her something to complain about. Aunt Earnestine sniffed again and said, "Thank you."

"Oh, you're welcome."

Aunt Earnestine said, "I'm glad you've lost your talent for throwing things around."

"Oh, I haven't lost my talent for it. Why, I could have swirled that jacket around a couple of times like this"—she waved one arm over her head—"and then let go. It would've landed on a peg."

"Disgusting," said Aunt Earnestine. She thrust her bag into Ida's hand. "Here, put this away, too."

"For purses," said Ida, "I use an underhand shot," and before Aunt Earnestine could protest, Ida drew way back, bending her knees as if she were bowling, and threw Aunt Earnestine's purse across the room. It landed in a pan of gravy on top of the stove.

"Oh, my goodness," said Ida. "I meant for it to go onto that little table against the wall." Randall knew she'd meant for it to land exactly where it did.

"You haven't changed, after all!" said Aunt Earnestine. She went across the room and lifted her purse off the top of the gravy. "It's ruined!"

"Oh, that's all right," said Ida. "It'll only take me a minute to whip up another panful."

"It's the bag I'm concerned about," said Aunt Earnestine, "not the gravy!"

Ida took the bag and examined it. "Well, it'll still hold your money. Ain't that all purses are for?"

"No, it's not *all* they're for," snapped Aunt Earnestine. "Haven't you ever heard of fashion?"

Ida laughed loudly. "Why, we know all about fashion up here in the mountains." She dampened a cloth and began dabbing at the purse. Randall knew that she'd soon have it looking good as new. "Why, the dry goods store in town keeps us up-to-date with high

styles. All you have to do is go past their show window and you can't help knowing what's the latest
thing. Right now, for instance, they're showing off a
pair of red-and-white-striped lounging pajamas." She
paused, giving Aunt Earnestine a chance to comment. When she didn't say anything, Ida continued.
"Have lounging pajamas hit your neighborhood yet?
If not, you'll just have to buy that pair in the show
window and introduce some *real* fashion to the folks
there!"

"Lounging pajamas are decadent," Aunt Earnestine said.

Before Ida could answer, the door from the back
porch burst open and the twins rushed inside. The
turkey followed them into the kitchen.

Randall thought for a moment that Aunt Earnestine would be sick. "What?" she gasped. "What's
that?"

"It's a turkey," said Ida Early. "You mean you've
never seen a turkey?"

"Of course I've seen a turkey!" snapped Aunt Earnestine. "But not in anybody's house!"

Dewey said proudly, "It's our Thanksgiving turkey," and Clay added, "It's real smart."

Aunt Earnestine said emphatically, "The proper
place for a Thanksgiving turkey is on the table."

The turkey hopped onto the hearth, and from there jumped, with one flap of its wings, onto the table.

"See how smart he is!" said Ida. "He heard you say that a turkey belongs on the table!"

"I meant *roasted*!" shouted Aunt Earnestine.

"Oh, now you've hurt his feelings," said Ida. "Oh, my goodness! He looks so sad." The turkey didn't look any different from the way he'd ever looked, but the twins rushed over and started petting it as if it were about to die. And Frizzy, the frizzled hen, who'd never been in the house in her life, flew from the doorway onto the table alongside the turkey. She started making little clucking noises as if she were trying to console it, too.

Randall wished the turkey would say something, but maybe it was best not to spring too many surprises on Aunt Earnestine at one time.

Love Blooms Forever

As soon as the table was cleared after lunch, Randall spread out pieces of his favorite jigsaw puzzle. It had more pieces and was harder to put together than either of his others, and he especially liked the picture: a pair of swans swimming on a big blue lake, with a castle in the background. Clay and Dewey sat beside him. They'd planned to go for a walk with Ida and Ellen but decided at the last minute they'd rather help with the puzzle.

The three boys had the kitchen to themselves until exactly two o'clock, when Aunt Earnestine came into the room and turned on the radio. Randall should have remembered. It was time for the one program she liked: a soap opera. Her timing was perfect: static noises, always present when the radio was warming up, ended just as a commercial for washing powders was over, and a smooth, low voice announced: "And now, listeners, it's time for *Love Blooms Forever.*"

Randall went on fitting pieces of the puzzle together, but the twins did not. He supposed they remembered how cross Aunt Earnestine had been last summer whenever anyone made the least bit of noise during "her program." Putting a puzzle together could hardly be described as noisy, but evidently the twins didn't want to risk even that. Still, he was surprised when they got down from the table, partway through the program, and went over and sat near Aunt Earnestine as if they were big fans of the soap opera, too.

Although Randall concentrated on the puzzle, he couldn't help half listening to the radio program. The story was about a poor, sweet, and very pretty young woman who'd been brought to the city by distant relatives. They pretended to be helping her but were actually using her as a servant. There was a handsome young man in the story, too, and he'd fallen for her but did not want to declare his love lest she not care for him. So the young woman let him know that she loved him truly by cutting out tiny heart-shaped pieces of paper and putting one on the edge of his plate whenever she served him anything. At first he hadn't caught on, but suddenly one day he realized that none of the other guests at a party had received a heart. At the end of the program the young man had gone out to price engagement rings. Randall thought it was the silliest thing he'd ever heard and was glad when Aunt Earnestine turned off the radio and went back to her room.

Soon Randall was engrossed in the puzzle again. The sky and the lake were the hardest to put together because all the pieces were blue and looked alike. He heard the twins across the room, whispering to each other. He turned around to see that they were at the bench near the fireplace. They had a pair of scissors and were whacking on construction paper they'd brought home from school.

"Aren't you going to help me with the puzzle?"

"We've got something else we have to do," said Clay, sounding as if it were an urgent task.

When Ida came in, they barely greeted her, which wasn't like them. She took off her sweater and walked out to the center of the room, and with a wink at Randall threw it toward the hatrack. Of course, it landed on a peg. Usually the twins would have run to fetch it and begged her to do the trick again. This time they didn't look up. "My goodness, fellows!" said Ida. "What's going on over there that's so important?"

"Nothing," said Clay.

Dewey added, "We're just playing."

Randall started to say, "They're cutting out valentines here on Thanksgiving," but decided there was no need to tease them. "Where's Ellen?" he asked.

"She stopped by the henhouse to gather the eggs," said Ida, sitting down beside him. Immediately she found a crucial piece of the sky that had eluded him.

After Ellen had brought in the eggs and put them in the wire basket on top of the icebox, she helped with the puzzle, too, and soon it was finished. The twins came over to look at it.

Ellen said, "I love that picture."

"Me, too," said Ida. "It reminds me of the castle where I used to live when I was a princess. In fact, I think it's the same one."

"Is that where you were living when you scared the dragon?" asked Dewey.

"The very place!" said Ida. "See that window on the side of the tower? That's where I was sitting, just minding my business, when that ol' dragon stuck his head inside and spit fiery bolts at me. I slipped down the back way and came out right down here where you see this gate"—she tapped the spot on the puzzle—"and sneaked around and grabbed him by his hind legs and slung him into the lake, right about where those swans are swimming."

"Did he drown?"

"No, but he sure got his fire put out," said Ida. "But come on, it's time for us to see to the afternoon chores. Then we must get ready for tonight. That new preacher, what's-his-name, is coming, and your Aunt Earnestine's here, and it's Thanksgiving night. It'll be a festive occasion."

Dewey and Clay looked at each other and giggled. "Yes," said Clay. "It'll be festive."

Aunt Earnestine scolded Mr. Sutton when he arrived home from work. "You shouldn't have to work such long hours, and certainly you shouldn't have worked today."

"Well," said Mr. Sutton, "we had some lumber on hand that didn't know today was Thanksgiving. It had to be seen to, but don't worry. I'm paid well, considering the times, and lucky to have a job. Anyway, I'm to get off earlier for the next few days."

Brother Preston arrived then, and Randall was glad. It would stop Aunt Earnestine from nagging at his father, for a while at least.

After greeting everyone and being introduced to Aunt Earnestine, the minister was invited to sit by the fire. "Come on around," said Mr. Sutton, "and pull up a chair." He offered him the biggest rocker.

"This looks good to me," said Brother Preston, sitting down on the big bench near the fireplace. Clay and Dewey rushed to sit on each side of him. They looked as if they were guarding him, thought Randall, who was helping Ida and Ellen with the meal.

Mr. Sutton called, "Hey, over there! This is a holiday! How about singing for us?"

Ellen said, "We're busy putting our supper on the table."

"Can't you sing and work at the same time?"

Ida answered, "Sure we can!" and she led off with "These Two-Dollar Shoes Hurt My Feet." She had been teaching Ellen and Randall to harmonize, and they joined in. At the end of each verse Ida yodeled loudly.

Mr. Sutton cheered when the song was finished. "Encore!" he called, but Aunt Earnestine said, "I think that's enough for now."

Randall, Ellen, and Ida grinned at each other; they'd have been surprised if she'd liked the song.

Soon the meal was ready, and while everyone was gathering around the table, Clay told Brother Preston, "Ida set the table." Randall wondered why Clay considered this something to report; Ida often set the table. Then Randall, standing back of his place between Aunt Earnestine and their guest, looked down at Brother Preston's place and saw immediately what the twins were up to. There in the corner of the plate in front of the preacher was a cut-out heart made from red paper. It was about the size of a quarter.

There was nothing special about the dishes in the Sutton household, and not many of them matched each other. Most of the plates were white, although one had a flowered design, another had a pink band around its edge, and another had a gray-and-red border. At a glance, the plate in front of Brother Preston looked as if the small heart, or valentine, were part of its design.

The minister stood back of his chair and looked down at the table. "My goodness! What have we here?" he said, obviously delighted.

The twins beamed.

Mr. Sutton looked to see what the minister was talking about. "Oh, that's something special from Ida!" he said, and Randall thought, Surely they haven't got Pa in on this, too.

"Well, I'll have to learn her secret," said Brother Preston, and Randall realized that the preacher had been admiring the platter of tomatoes near his plate.

The slices were as big as saucers, and they were garnished with sprigs of parsley and rings of sweet pepper.

"She picked the tomatoes just ahead of frost," explained Mr. Sutton, "and wrapped them some way—or talked to them!—and they ripened."

Ida, bringing a salt shaker to the table, said, "But we didn't have frost till late this year."

"Still," said Mr. Sutton, "this is the first time we've ever had homegrown tomatoes at Thanksgiving. But come on, everybody, let's have a seat and get at these vittles!"

After everyone was seated, Randall reached over and stuck his fork in a peach pickle that was in a dish near him. Ida had made the pickles in late summer, and these were from the first jar that had been opened. Randall couldn't think of many things that were better than peach pickles.

Aunt Earnestine swatted the back of his hand. "Before the blessing?" she asked.

Randall knew better. He didn't know why he'd reached for the pickle. Now he didn't know whether to return it to the dish or go ahead and put it on his plate. His father smiled at him and said, "Let's bow our heads." Randall eased the pickle onto his plate as the blessing was being asked.

While the food was being passed around, the twins

could hardly serve their own plates for looking to see what Brother Preston was going to do with the heart on his plate. Randall wondered the same thing, but it didn't keep him from helping himself generously from the dishes before him. On the big platter that in other years had held turkey there was a tuna fish and rice dish that had been shaped into a big ring, with a cheese sauce in the middle. Around the outside of the ring there were apple halves that had been poached in syrup. There were red ones and green ones; the red ones were cinnamon-flavored, the green ones were mint. Other dishes included spinach from the garden, topped with slices of boiled eggs; string beans; candied sweet potatoes with raisins; fried okra; fresh pears from the tree in the backyard stuffed with a mixture of homemade cottage cheese and nuts; huckleberry muffins; and corn bread.

When the tuna ring was passed to Brother Preston, he piled a heaping serving of it smack onto the heart that was on his plate, and put a generous amount of cheese sauce on top. No doubt, he'd discover the heart at the end of the meal, thought Randall, imagining how bedraggled it would look with food stains on it.

Conversation got under way soon about the Depression and whether the hard times might at last be getting better. Naturally, everyone hoped so. "There's no easy way to tough out the lean years," said Mr. Sutton. "You just do the best you can, whether you're in the country or in the city."

"True," agreed Aunt Earnestine. "But in the country you stand a chance of growing more of your own food. For example, this is a nourishing repast."

"And delicious," said Brother Preston. "It's just about the best meal I ever ate."

Aunt Earnestine looked around the table. "Yet I don't see anything but the raisins in the candied sweet potatoes that you didn't or couldn't raise yourself."

"The tuna fish," said Clay. "We didn't raise the tuna fish, Aunt Earnestine."

Aunt Earnestine smiled. "Yes, of course. But I still say that bad times are worse if you have to buy everything." Randall knew that Aunt Earnestine might not be able to grow her own food, but he expected she was better able than many people to buy what she needed. He'd heard his father say that her husband, who'd died so long ago that Randall couldn't remember him, had left her some money.

Partway through the meal, Brother Preston began to sputter. Everyone looked at him, and after a few seconds he swallowed as if he were almost choking. Afterward he said nothing except "Pardon me," although a strange look came over his face. Randall noticed that he'd eaten the food from the side of the plate where the heart had been—and nothing, not even the heart, was left. The twins looked alarmed. Randall doubted anyone had ever died from swallowing a small scrap of paper, and he thought of the soap opera and almost laughed out loud. This would teach the twins to play Cupid!

When it was time for dessert, Ida asked, "Who'll help me serve the pie?"

Clay and Dewey sprang to their feet. "We will!" they shouted.

"Good boys," said Mr. Sutton. "Thanksgiving has put you in a helpful mood." Usually the twins were interested in eating dessert, not serving it.

The dish was mincemeat pie, with filling that Ida had made, surrounded by flaky crust that was one of her many specialties. She cut the pie and put pieces of it onto small plates spread out on the work table near the window. "This one's for your father," she told the twins, meaning that it was a bit larger than some of the others. "And this one's especially for Brother Preston." The twins scurried back and forth with the desserts.

"This one's from Ida to you!" said Clay as he put a plate in front of the preacher. Dewey stood back of him; then they hurried to their own places.

Everyone but the twins began to eat the pie. They appeared more interested in whether or not the preacher ate his. Then Randall saw it: the heart-shaped cut-out, slightly bigger than the first one, in the middle of the wedge of pie that had been served Brother Preston. Randall's first thought was, Well, at least he's not apt to eat this one. But then he worried: what if the poor man thought the heart was made from some kind of pie crust, tinted and cut as a decoration? He hated to get the twins in trouble, but on the other hand, it wouldn't be right to let their guest make another mistake about the paper. He was trying to decide whether to say something or not when Brother Preston took his fork and lifted the heart onto the edge of the saucer beneath his coffee cup, looking around a bit sheepishly at the same time. He could certainly see, like the hero of the soap opera, thought Randall, that no one else had been served a valentine.

Clay asked, "How do you like your dessert, Brother Preston?" and Dewey reminded him, "Ida said that piece was just for you!"

"Yes, I know," said the minister. Randall couldn't tell if he was flattered or confused until Brother Preston grinned at the twins and then at Ida. Randall supposed he was pleased. In any event, the twins looked enormously satisfied.

Making Up Verses,
Popping Up Corn

J.C., his little brother, Archie, and their mother had all been sick, so on the Saturday after Thanksgiving Ida made an extra pan of biscuits and a big pot of soup to send them.

"It might help with their supper," she told Randall, who took it to them.

Mr. Gilson, J.C.'s father, came to the door. "My folks are better," he said, "but maybe you'd better not come in. I'd hate for your family to have a siege of it, too. But you tell Ida how much we appreciate all the good things she's made for us this week." Randall hadn't known that she'd made anything else.

"Yes, sir, I'll tell her," promised Randall, and he started away, after telling Mr. Gilson that he hoped J.C. and everybody else would soon be well.

On the way home he thought again of last year at this time. Off and on, all day long, memories of that day kept coming back to him. The whole family had spent the Saturday after Thanksgiving in Chattanooga; it had been his mother's idea. They'd gone to Rock City on Lookout Mountain and then to a picture show in town. There were hot dogs afterward and cider at a roadside stand on the way home.

In the backyard Randall stopped at the woodpile and chopped a stack of kindling for starting fires. Then he went about his other chores. He'd fed the pigs and was shelling corn for the chickens when he saw Ida heading out the path to the barn to do the milking. They waved to each other.

Ida had taken over the milking chores from Randall. In return, he built the fires every morning—a job he liked better. He usually woke up early, anyway, and he didn't mind the task. Of course, on really cold mornings he'd be willing to trade that chore for something else. Still, somebody had to do it.

Often the twins followed Ida whenever she went to the barn, but this time they'd stayed in the kitchen. They were popping corn with Ellen. They weren't allowed to pop corn by themselves because of the fire hazard. The kernels, placed in a wire box on the end of a long handle, had to be shaken over fiery hot coals that were pulled toward the front of the hearth. More than one fire in the mountains had been started because someone had been careless during a corn-popping session.

When Randall had filled the big box in the kitchen with stovewood and had put extra logs onto the porch for burning in the open fire, he took off his jacket and settled in for the night. He was sprinkling salt onto a big bowl of corn that Ellen and Clay had popped when Mr. Sutton came in from work.

"Few things smell better than fresh-popped corn," said Mr. Sutton, taking a handful from the bowl Randall held out to him. "Or taste better." He sat down on the bench between Ellen and Randall and slipped off his shoes. "Aah! That feels good."

Randall said, "I thought Reverend Preston was coming home with you for supper."

"No, we didn't exactly take him on as a boarder, although we'll be as neighborly as we can. He's eating somewhere else tonight."

Clay turned to Randall. "You're not supposed to call him Reverend Preston."

"Why not?"

" 'Cause," said Clay, "just grown-ups are supposed to say Reverend. And you're not grown."

Mr. Sutton said, "He's nearly grown." He put an arm over Randall's shoulder and added, "Aren't you, Sport?"

"Almost," agreed Randall.

"I don't think there's any rule about exactly what to call a minister," said Mr. Sutton. "I'd guess that children are usually more comfortable saying Mister or Brother. Somehow I am, myself. But a lot of people say Reverend. Call him whatever you choose."

Clay said, "Maybe we'll call him Rev!" He and Dewey giggled.

"No, that might sound disrespectful."

Ellen said, "You could call him Preacher Preston. That has a nice ring to it."

"So it has," said Mr. Sutton. "I'd say it's downright euphonious."

The twins asked at the same time, "What's euphonious?" The bigger any word they didn't know, the quicker they were to ask its meaning.

"It means something's pleasant sounding," said Mr. Sutton. "But on second thought, I don't know but what Preacher Preston sounds more like a tongue twister."

The twins didn't have to ask what a tongue twister

was. They could say all of "Peter Piper picked a peck of pickled peppers" quicker than anyone else in the family—and without making a mistake.

"Let's write a verse of some sort," said Ellen. Recently she'd been trying her hand at writing poems. "Let's see: Preacher Preston pressed his—" She scratched her head. "What would he press?"

"His pants," said Randall. "What else would Preacher Preston press?"

"Preacher Preston pressed his pants," said Ellen. "No, that doesn't sound right. Keep thinking." She went over to the shelf near the window and brought back her notebook and opened it to a fresh sheet of paper. After scribbling for a few moments, she asked, "Well, how about this: Preacher Preston prayed for progress."

"Good!" said Dewey. "That's real good, Ellen."

"Come on, everybody," Ellen said. "What does he pray for?"

Mr. Sutton said, "I think we could work it out if somebody'd pop one more batch of corn to give us strength."

Dewey, with Randall's help, filled the popper and shook it over fresh coals.

"All right," said Ellen. "What'd he pray for?"

Mr. Sutton said, "Well, lots of times in their prayers at church ministers say things like, Keep us free, O Lord, from strife and discord."

Clay said, "That's not euphonious!"

"Good for you, Clay," said Mr. Sutton. "And no, I guess it's not."

"I have an idea," said Dewey. "Preacher Preston prayed for snow."

Randall knew that in their bedtime prayers the last few nights, the twins had prayed for the same thing. "That has possibilities," he said. "How about:

> "Preacher Preston prayed for snow;
> God said, 'No.' "

"Nope," said Ellen, busily making notes. "That won't do either, but we're getting there. I'm onto it now. Just give me a minute."

While she was thinking, Mr. Sutton and the boys helped themselves to popcorn. Ellen was too busy with her writing to take even one mouthful. She scribbled more lines in her notebook, erased them, and wrote something else. At last she said, "Here it is! Is everybody ready?"

"Ready and waiting," Mr. Sutton teased.

"Stand in front of us," said Dewey, "like you're on a stage."

Ellen laughed. "Why not?" she said, getting to her

feet. She stepped onto the middle of the rug in front of the fire and read:

"Preacher Preston prayed for progress:
  'Keep us free from strife and pain.'
Preacher Preston prayed for sunshine,
  What he got instead was rain!"

Randall couldn't remember when he'd heard his father laugh so heartily. He and the twins thought the verse was funny, too, and were laughing when Aunt Earnestine came into the room. "What's so funny?" she asked.

It was almost as if a cold draft had swept across the kitchen. Nobody said a word. Randall knew Aunt Earnestine wouldn't think their verse-writing was funny.

Mr. Sutton said, "Oh, we were just having a little discussion of poetry." He nudged Randall and added, "It was our cultural event for the day. Wasn't it, fellows?" He winked at the twins.

"Yes," said Dewey, and Clay said, "Ellen makes up poems. Don't you, Ellen?"

"Don't put all the blame on me," said Ellen. "I had some help with that last one, remember?"

Aunt Earnestine said, "Maybe you'd read us one of your offerings now so that I could enjoy it, too?" Randall doubted Ellen would read the verse, and he hoped the twins wouldn't try to recite any of it from memory.

Ellen said, "Oh, all right," and she turned back a page in her notebook.

The twins looked as if they were going to burst out laughing before a word was read. Ellen looked at them and then seemed uncertain. "First I must tell you, this one's not a funny one, okay?"

The twins looked puzzled.

"Really," said Ellen, "maybe I'd better not read it. I just thought—"

Clay said, "It's okay. We know how to act if it's not funny," and Dewey said, "Yes, we know," and their smiles disappeared at once. If something serious was to be offered, they were set for it.

"Well," said Ellen, still standing in front of the fire, "this one's not finished. In fact, it's barely begun, but since it's about all of us, I'll read what I have. It's called 'Last Year We Were Happy,' and it starts off:

"We went to Chattanooga,
    Our family, for the day,
  This year we are happy, too,
    But in a different way."

No one said anything for a long time. Aunt Earnestine hadn't been with the family on the outing last year, but she'd heard about it. "Yes," she said, "I know how special that day was to all of you."

Mr. Sutton, his voice more gentle than ever, said, "I can't tell you how many times today I've thought of that trip. It was on the Saturday after Thanksgiving Day."

"Mamma thought it up," said Randall.

"I remember," said Mr. Sutton. "And I don't know who had the most fun."

"We did!" said Clay.

"Yes," said Mr. Sutton. "You did. And I did. And your mother did. We all had a good time, didn't we? It was a special day, all right."

Ellen sat down again on the bench, and Mr. Sutton pulled her to him and kissed her on the forehead. "It's a nice poem," he said, just as they heard Ida coming up the steps of the back porch. "Of course, it's not the same without your mother, but she'd be glad that we're together . . . and healthy . . . and growing. You're right, we're happy in a different kind of way."

Ida burst into the room then with the milking bucket. "How about this?" she said, bringing over the bucket to show that it was brimming full. "That's one smart cow! Nobody told her that I was thinking about making boiled custard tonight if she'd just give more milk than ever."

60

"We did!" said Dewey.

"Did what?"

"Told the cow. We told her you'd said you *might* make us some boiled custard tonight."

Bigger than Mountains

While the twins and Ida listened to *The Saturday Night Barn Dance* on the radio, Randall read. Ellen had gone to bed early, and Aunt Earnestine and Mr. Sutton sat by the fire and chatted.

When the program ended, Ida told Clay and Dewey that she'd put them to bed. "But we don't want to go." said Clay. They ran over and climbed onto their father's lap. He teased them as he hugged them to him. "I know two little boys who never want to go to bed." Then he kissed them and told them to go with Ida. "If you stay up, you'll get cross," he said when Clay insisted it was still early. He added good-naturedly, "You've had too much barn dance!"

As they walked away, Aunt Earnestine said, "They've had too much boiled custard." She hadn't approved of everyone being served a second helping of it at supper.

The book Randall was reading was not very interesting, and although he tried to concentrate on it, he realized that he was paying almost as much attention to the conversation his father and Aunt Earnestine were having.

Aunt Earnestine asked, "What would Clarrie think if she could see that the household is being run in such a carefree manner?"

Randall smiled. Carefree. That was Ida all right. Still, it worried him that Aunt Earnestine kept saying, "What would Clarrie think?" Clarrie had been his mother, and he knew that if his father was ever convinced that she'd have disapproved of the way the family was being looked after, he'd be upset. And he'd do something about it.

Randall admitted that his mother had been different from Ida. *Everybody* was different from Ida. His mother had had a sense of humor, but it was a gentle kind; she never did outrageous and funny things the way Ida sometimes did. And it was true that she took more pains in housekeeping. He looked at a bouquet of wild asters that Ida had put in a fruit jar. No doubt his mother would have arranged them carefully in a pretty vase. Still, he believed that she and Ida would have liked each other.

When his mother died, Randall had doubted anyone in the family would ever be happy again. Now, thanks to Ida, no one dwelled long on sadness. Sometimes he wondered if he was being disloyal to his mother in liking so much the person who'd taken her place in many ways. But he knew that was dumb.

He put down his book and excused himself from the kitchen. In the room that he shared with the twins, he sat down on the end of his bed and listened to the lullaby Ida was singing to them. When it was finished, Dewey said, "We love you, Ida, just the way we loved Mamma."

Ida said, "No, now, I'm not your mamma. And you can't count on me being here forever."

Clay said, "Mamma wasn't here forever either."

"All the same, you must remember her as your rightful mamma. I'm just filling in for a little while."

Clay said, "I'm glad Aunt Earnestine's not filling in."

Ida started from the room, but she turned back and said softly, "We must be nice to your aunt. Tonight she looked as if she might be coming down with something."

In the morning after breakfast Mr. Sutton sat at the big table in the kitchen, the Sunday paper spread out before him. He read the comic strips aloud. Ida and the twins pulled their chairs near to look and to listen. Randall and Ellen, washing and drying the breakfast dishes, listened, too.

Ida laughed more than anyone else at the funny parts, and often she'd make comments. "Poor Little Orphan Annie!" she'd say when Annie was in trouble. Then she'd pat the twins and say, "But don't you worry—everything'll come out all right." Or she'd say, "Ain't that just like Moon Mullins!" She and the twins spoke of comic strip characters as if they were old friends.

When he'd finished reading *The Katzenjammer Kids*, Mr. Sutton folded the paper and put it aside.

"But that's not all!" said Clay.

"We'll finish them this afternoon," said his father. "It's almost time for us to be off to Sunday school."

"I think I'll stay home today," said Clay, which surprised Randall. The family always went to Sunday school—and to morning worship service afterward.

"I think I'll stay home, too," said Dewey, which didn't surprise anyone. The twins usually were together in what they would—and wouldn't—do. "A double force," their father called them.

"You'd better go with us," said Mr. Sutton. "Everybody needs a little religion to get along in life."

"Ida doesn't have any religion," said Clay. "And she gets along."

"Who said I didn't have any religion?" asked Ida. "Why, I don't suppose you'd ever guess that—"

"I would," said Dewey. "I'd guess it, Ida."

"What would you guess?"

"That once upon a time you had more religion than anybody in the whole big world."

"How ever did you know?" asked Ida.

"I just guessed," said Dewey.

Ida leaned over and kissed him on the forehead. "No," she said, "but just because I don't go to church doesn't mean I'm not a believer in God. I ain't as sure about every little detail as some folks make out like they are, but maybe we're meant to be mystified. I've come across a number of different people who've had a number of different views, all of 'em claiming to've got theirs from the Bible."

"They can't all be right," said Clay, "if they're different."

"Exactly," said Ida. "And who's to say who's right? So I try to keep an open mind about it. Still, I've got religion— I know for certain there's something bigger than me."

"Bigger than you?" said Clay. "No, I don't think so. I don't think anybody's bigger than you."

"A giant would be bigger," said Dewey. "Are you a lady giant, Ida?"

"Well," said Ida, "maybe *nobody* is bigger than I am, but *something* must surely be."

"The mountains are bigger," said Dewey. "They're bigger than you are, Ida."

"That's right. That's good thinking, Dewey, and it's what I meant. The mountains are bigger, and whoever made the mountains must've been bigger."

"The sky is bigger than you are, too," said Dewey. "And trees."

Clay said, "Not *all* trees. Ida's bigger than the wild plum out by the pasture gate." He turned to his father and added, "So we'll just stay home with Ida. She has all the religion we need."

Mr. Sutton laughed but said firmly, "No, you must come along. But why not invite Ida to go with you? I've asked her to come to our grown-ups' class, but she's declined. Maybe she'd go with you and help your teachers in the children's classes." Randall had heard Aunt Earnestine say, "Well, if she's not a churchgoing person she certainly should not be in a position to influence your children." Maybe that was what his father was thinking about now.

"I'd better stay here and get Sunday dinner cooked," said Ida.

Ellen said, "But you've cooked most of it already. And I'll help when we get home."

"But somebody should stay here with Aunt Earnestine," said Ida.

"No," said Mr. Sutton. "She's gone back to bed because of a headache. She'll be all right."

Randall said, "Brother Preston'll be there. Wouldn't you like to see him again?"

Ida said flatly, "Invite him home for dinner."

"I already did," said Mr. Sutton. "But he's eating somewhere else. He said he might see us in the afternoon, though."

Finally Ida was persuaded to go to Sunday school with the family. "I'll put on my Sunday duds," she said, heading toward her room.

Randall wondered if she still had the pale green dress that she'd bought in September when she'd tried to be more like other women. She'd never looked comfortable in it; overalls suited her better.

A few moments later Ida came back into the room.

She wore the riding pants and jacket she'd had on when she'd returned to the Suttons. Ida had left in early October and had stayed away nearly two months. It had seemed even longer. Then, just when it was almost certain that Aunt Earnestine would come back to look after the family, Ida had ridden into the yard on the back of a motorcycle. She'd caught a ride up the mountain.

Randall hoped nobody at Sunday school would tell Ida that she shouldn't wear riding pants to church. Besides, just because none of the other women wore them didn't mean it wasn't all right. He was glad Preacher Thaxton wouldn't be there. Preacher Thaxton had thought almost everything was wrong. He'd preached about such things as what a sin it was to dance, or for women to cut their hair short or wear makeup. Once there had been a whole sermon on how wicked it was for women to smoke. Randall had wondered why it was wicked for women to smoke if it wasn't the same for men.

On the way across the parking lot at church, the Suttons waved at Brother Preston, who was standing with a group of men out front. In his dark suit, white shirt, and tie, Randall thought he bore little resemblance to the man who'd eaten supper with them twice during the week. Randall half-expected him to yell, "Howdy!" across the church yard, but he didn't.

Mr. Sutton stopped to speak to a friend who was just arriving, and the children and Ida went toward the front entrance. As they passed the group of men with Brother Preston, Randall noticed that all of them looked at Ida as if they'd never seen a riding outfit.

Clay called, "Hello, Brother Preston!" and Dewey said, "Good morning, Brother Preston!"

Brother Preston only nodded.

"Reckon why he didn't say something to us?" asked Dewey.

"Couldn't you tell?" said Ida. "His tie was choking him, that's why!" The twins laughed as they went into the Sunday school room.

Loaves and Fishes

Mrs. Todd was the head of the children's classes. Ellen introduced Ida to her, and the twins beamed as proudly as if they were showing off a Christmas tree. Mrs. Todd looked a bit surprised—anyone meeting Ida for the first time looked surprised—but then she greeted her warmly. "I'm delighted that you're here," she said. "I've just learned that Mrs. Melton will be away for several weeks. She has that terrible strain of flu that's going around. Maybe you'd take her class?"

"Take it where?" asked Ida.

Mrs. Todd smiled. "Just visit with the children.

Read them today's Bible story. Or tell it to them. And enjoy being together."

"Thank you," said Ida, "but I'm only visiting."

Dewey said, "It's our class, Ida," and Clay added, "You can visit and teach, too."

"It would be nice if you would," said Mrs. Todd.

"All right," said Ida. "I suppose I could give it a shot." She winked at Randall. He could imagine her spending the class period teaching the primary children how to improve their aim. Maybe they'd make paper airplanes or spitballs.

After an opening song the roll was called. Then Mrs. Todd asked if anyone had had a birthday during the week, and Jane Elton raised her hand. She was invited to the front of the room while everyone sang "Happy Birthday" to her. Then Mrs. Todd talked about Thanksgiving, which was just over, and how food, in celebration of the harvest, was a part of it. "Our Bible lesson for today includes a story about food also," she said, "but your teachers will tell it to you. Why don't we go to our classes now?"

The twins, one holding to each hand, led Ida away. Their class was held in a small room in back. Ellen went in another direction. Randall and his classmates stayed in the main room, and Mrs. Caldwell, their teacher, told them the story of how Jesus had fed so many people on five pieces of bread and two fishes that one boy had brought for his lunch. It had been a favorite story with the Sutton children when their mother used to tell it to them. Mrs. Caldwell did not make a very interesting story of it now, and Randall was glad when the period ended.

Brother Preston came into the room just after everyone had gathered for the closing part of the program. "I'd like to take a few minutes to see if the boys and girls have learned their lesson for today," he said. Randall thought, He sounds exactly like Preacher Thaxton. "Who can tell me what it was about?"

Blake Gilmore, sitting next to Ellen, raised his hand. Blake always liked to answer questions. Instead of calling on him, Brother Preston looked at Ida and the children from the primary class. Randall doubted they'd gotten around to talking about the lesson, so he raised his hand. Brother Preston looked as if he were about to call on him, but then he said, "Suppose someone in the primary group tells me about it. Maybe one of the twins?"

"Which one?" asked Clay.

"Your brother," said the preacher, sounding the least bit annoyed.

"Yes, I can tell you what it was about," said Dewey.

He stopped there as if he'd answered the question.

"Well, go ahead. Tell us."

Ellen looked as alarmed as Randall felt. Then Dewey said, "It was about five loaves of bread, only they were more like biscuits, and two fishes, and how Jesus stretched that little dab to feed a whole crowd of folks."

"The multitude," corrected the minister. "According to the Scriptures, Jesus broke the loaves and fishes and gave them to his disciples, and they in turn gave out the food to the multitude. Now who can tell us how many people were fed?"

"More than five thousand men, besides women and children," answered Clay. Randall knew that no fault could be found with that answer.

"And who knows how much was left over after the multitude had been fed?"

Every hand in the primary class went up. "That was the best part!" said Jordie Williams, who was sitting between Clay and Dewey.

"All right, suppose you tell us."

"Well," said Jordie, "there were twelve basketsful of regular table scraps."

"Fragments from the loaves and fishes," corrected Brother Preston.

"Yes, sir," said Jordie, "and a bucket of peanut

shells, and a barrel of apple peelings, and a stalk of bananas that had barely been touched."

Lisa Madison added, "And a wagonload of watermelon rinds and half of a big birthday cake with red candles on it."

"Where did you hear that?"

"She told us about it," said Lisa, pointing at Ida.

Brother Preston asked crossly, "Did you?"

"Why, that's the way I've always heard it," said Ida, sounding so innocent, thought Randall, that no one would think she'd ever made up anything in her life. "You mean that's not the way *you've* always heard it?"

"No, it's not! And that's not the way it appears in the Bible."

"Well, I reckon it just got sort of added to along the line," said Ida. "Most of my Bible training was from hearing stories instead of reading 'em."

Jordie nudged Ida. "Tell him about the elephants coming out and putting on a show after the scraps— I mean fragments—had been taken up."

"Yes, do!" Lisa said excitedly. "And the buggy race, and how all the horses turned out to be camels. We want to hear it again!"

Brother Preston looked horrified, but the primary children were all smiling up at Ida.

Chief Nurse and Stablemaid

By Sunday afternoon Aunt Earnestine was running a high fever. Dewey asked, "Does that mean she won't go home tomorrow?"

"It means she won't go home for at least two weeks," said Mr. Sutton, "maybe longer." The doctor, who came out at midday, had said that she had flu, the dreaded type that was going around. Two people in the far end of the county had died from it. "It's highly contagious," said Mr. Sutton, and before Clay or Dewey could ask what "contagious" meant, he explained, "That means it's catching, and we must all do everything possible not to get it. Ida will be the chief nurse, and I'll help out when I'm home, but you children must stay out of the room, do you hear?" That would be easy, thought Randall. Nobody wanted to visit Aunt Earnestine. Still, he was sorry she was sick. "And try to be quiet," added his father. That would not be so easy.

Mr. Sutton went back to see about Aunt Earnestine, and Ida pulled a white apron from the bottom drawer of a cabinet and put it on over her overalls. Then she took a big dinner napkin and folded it to look like a nurse's cap, pinned it together with safety pins, and threw it toward the ceiling. When it came down, she caught it on her head. It landed at a jaunty angle. "There!" she said, turning around as if she were modeling the outfit. "I don't suppose any of you would ever guess that—"

"I would," said Dewey. "I'd guess it," and Ida asked what he'd guess.

"That you were once upon a time chief nurse for the whole big world."

Ida appeared shocked. "Somebody told you! Somebody must've told you, or you'd never have guessed it!" She went on to tell about the important people she'd nursed back to health. There'd been presidents, movie stars, and ball players. "And the King of England," she added. "Why, he refused to get sick if he couldn't have me wait on him. He'd send a big ship just to fetch me."

Mr. Sutton came back into the kitchen. "Earnestine's sleeping," he said. "I'll listen for her if the rest of you want to get outdoors while the weather's so nice."

Outside, the twins wanted to go for a walk in the woods, but Ida said she'd better stay close to the house in case she was needed. She pulled a deck of cards out of her pocket and said, "But I tell you what I *will* do. I'll teach you how to play blackjack."

"What's blackjack?" asked Clay.

"It's a game we big-time gamblers like," explained Ida. "But we'll just play for fun, okay? Let's see, what could we use instead of money?"

"How about chinaberries?" asked Randall. There was a small tree loaded with them out near the road.

"No," said Ellen, "they smell bad. Let's use acorns."

"Good idea!" agreed Ida, and when everyone had gathered twenty acorns each, they sat down on the ground and Ida explained the game.

Randall was surprised at how simple it was. In a story he'd read last summer, a boy's father had lost all his money playing blackjack in a casino in Europe. Somehow he'd have thought a game in which a fortune could be lost would be a little bit complicated. In any event, it was fun. He and Ellen had offered to help the twins, but they'd learned as quickly as anyone else. Both twins were good at arithmetic, and it was only necessary to add to twenty-one in order to play.

Once, when Clay finished his turn at dealing and had beaten everybody, he said, "Blackjack is my favorite game."

Dewey said, "Tiddlywinks is my favorite." Nobody had ever beaten Dewey at Tiddlywinks.

"Well, my favorite is Monopoly," said Ellen. The game was almost a craze with her and Randall's friends.

"When are you gonna buy a set of it?" asked Clay.

"Oh, sooner or later," said Ellen.

"Or never," added Randall. They'd managed to save enough money once to buy the game, but the store had been sold out. They'd bought something else instead. "We're gonna die of old age before we save up enough money ever again."

"Don't say that," Ellen scolded. "We've just got to have us a Monopoly set!"

"Meanwhile, we play blackjack," said Ida, starting to deal a round of cards. "This time ol' Ida's gonna mop up!"

Sure enough, she beat everyone on that hand, and Clay was not absolutely certain that blackjack was his favorite game after all. But it was Ellen who had the best luck from then on. After a while she'd won almost all the acorns, and Ida suggested that it was time to bring the game to a halt. "Why couldn't we all just pick up a handful of acorns and play longer?" asked Clay. "There are lots more on the ground."

"We'll do that some other time," said Ida. "All right, Ellen, deal one last hand."

Just as Ellen finished dealing the cards, a car drove into the yard. It parked on the side of the driveway, and Brother Preston and Mrs. Landis got out. Mrs. Landis's husband, who was not with them, was one of the officials of the church.

"What?" said Brother Preston when he came closer. "Are you playing cards on Sunday?" He could see that they were, thought Randall. With cards in front of each person, what else would they be playing?

"No," said Clay, "we're not playing cards." Randall was surprised. The twins often tried to talk their way out of trouble, but they never tried to get out of anything by lying. Clay added, "We're playing *blackjack*, not *cards*."

Ida laughed, and Randall said, "Blackjack and cards are the same thing."

"No," said Clay. "Old Maid and cards are the same thing."

"Never mind," said Brother Preston crossly. Then, as if he were reading from a rule book, he said, "Cards of any sort shall not be played on Sunday, not even Old Maid. And blackjack, a form of gambling, shall *never* be played."

"Why?" asked Clay.

"Because gambling is a sin."

Randall thought Ida would explain that in this instance it was only something to keep the children quiet while Aunt Earnestine rested, but she said firmly, "All life is a gamble."

Brother Preston couldn't have looked more surprised, thought Randall, if someone had hit him.

"I didn't mean to make you hot under the collar," said Ida. She reached into the bib pocket of her overalls and pulled out a nickel bag of Bull Durham smoking tobacco. "Here, roll yourself a cigarette. It'll help settle you down."

"I don't smoke."

Ida held out the bag of tobacco to Mrs. Landis. "What about you? Care for one?"

Mrs. Landis said pleasantly, "No, but thank you, anyway." Randall thought he detected a slight smile.

Ida rolled a cigarette, using only one hand.

"Smoking's not the best habit in the world, I admit," she said. "But maybe it's not the worst either." She struck a match on the seat of her overalls, lit the cigarette, and blew five perfect smoke rings in a row. Mrs. Landis definitely smiled then.

Mr. Sutton came into the yard. After he'd greeted the guests, he explained that Aunt Earnestine had flu. "You mustn't come in the house," he said, "but we could sit on the front porch."

"No," said Mrs. Landis, "we really shouldn't tarry. I'm taking Brother Preston around to visit some of the members. George had planned to, but he isn't feeling well."

Brother Preston said to Mr. Sutton, "I've just spoken to Ida and the children about the importance of keeping the Sabbath holy."

"Good," said Mr. Sutton. "And in this instance keeping it quiet. I'd say they've done a good job."

Randall was certain that Brother Preston was about to bring up the card game, but at that moment Frizzy stepped out from behind a clump of weeds nearby as if she'd been called.

"What a marvelous chicken!" said Mrs. Landis. "I've never seen one like it."

Clay said, "Lots of folks think she's funny-looking, but that's just 'cause she's different."

Dewey added, "We think Frizzy's pretty."

Mr. Sutton laughed. "On the other hand, some of us think Frizzy's lazy. She's been with us a long time, and she hasn't troubled herself to lay an egg yet!"

"But she has other talents," said Ida, holding her left arm straight out to the side and making a strange, clucking noise. Frizzy looked up immediately and flew onto Ida's arm. Perching there, she looked around as if she expected everyone to cheer. Even Brother Preston smiled.

Ida then made a funny, gobbling sound, and the turkey stepped out from behind the weeds, flapped its wings, and flew onto Ida's other arm.

Mrs. Landis clapped her hands. "Gracious goodness!" she said. "That's wonderful! You certainly have a way with animals."

Ida looked pleased, and Dewey said, "She used to be a lion tamer."

Mrs. Landis laughed.

"We must go," said Brother Preston, starting toward the car.

"No, wait a minute," said Mrs. Landis. "I've just had an idea." Then she looked at Ida. "I'm in charge of the Christmas program this year, and instead of a pageant, I'm thinking it might be nice to have a tableau, maybe combining it with some music."

Clay asked, "What's a tableau?"

Mrs. Landis explained that it was a scene posed by real people in costume. The Christmas one, she said, would be presented in front of the church and would be the manger scene. There'd be Joseph and the Virgin Mary at the manger, the three Wise Men nearby, and shepherds off to the side. "It would be even more effective to have real animals, too. The hen, for instance, could sit on the edge of the manger."

"What about a goat?" asked Clay.

"Perhaps," said Mrs. Landis. "But what would be perfect would be a cow and a donkey."

"We have a cow," said Dewey.

"But we don't have a donkey," added Clay.

Mr. Sutton said, "Moe Talbot has one. He said once he'd give it to anybody who could catch it. It's run wild in his pasture and swamp two or three years now."

"I could catch it," said Brother Preston, "but I wouldn't have time to work at getting it really tame."

"Ida could do that," said Clay.

"Do you suppose you could?" Mrs. Landis asked her.

Ida hesitated. "I've got lots of responsibilities around here, and I don't know."

"You'd be good at it," said Randall. He knew that Ida needed only a bit of urging.

"I ain't doubting I could train it if Brother Preston would bring it over here, but a donkey takes a little handling even after it's trained. Would somebody be in that . . . whatchamacallit . . ."

"Tableau," said Brother Preston.

"Yeah, but would anybody be in it who could make the donkey behave? Otherwise it might haul off and kick a Wise Man or the Virgin Mary or somebody."

"We'd work it out so that you'd be in the tableau," said Mrs. Landis. "Then you'd be right there to keep the animals under control. Who's to say there wasn't a stablemaid nearby when Jesus was born?"

"I am!" said Brother Preston. "There's no mention of it in the Bible."

Mrs. Landis said, "Oh, I don't think anyone would mind if we added a character to the scene."

"I'll help you out," said Ida enthusiastically. "I'll train the animals." Looking at Brother Preston, she added, "And I'll be the stablemaid."

The Donkey Chase

Aunt Earnestine's high fever continued, and she grew
weaker. The doctor came every afternoon to check
on her. "If you weren't doing such a good job of
looking after her," he told Ida, "I'd put her in the
hospital."

On Thursday, as the doctor was leaving, he looked
at the twins, who were sitting with Randall on the
steps. Randall realized later that it was probably the
fact that they were sitting, instead of out playing,
that caused the doctor to wonder if something was
wrong. After the doctor had taken their temperature

and examined their throats, he shook his head. They must be put to bed immediately.

In two days the twins were well. Whatever they'd had was over as quickly as it had begun. Their only complaint now was that they'd been allowed to miss such a short time from school.

Randall worried that Ida Early might catch the flu. She looked tired. He and Ellen helped with the chores around the house, but they weren't allowed in the sickroom. Ida could be heard in the night going to check on Aunt Earnestine, taking her a cup of hot tea or a glass of fruit juice. Whenever she had a coughing spell, Ida would hurry to fetch the cough syrup. The nights the twins had been sick, Randall doubted she'd gone to bed at all.

The first of the next week, the doctor quit coming to see Aunt Earnestine. Mr. Sutton told his family, "At last she's out of danger."

"Can she go home now?" asked Clay.

"No," said Mr. Sutton, "she's not strong enough for that. We'll keep her with us through Christmas at least."

The idea of Aunt Earnestine's visit lasting through Christmas did not cheer up anyone. The twins got up and went to bed without having to be told that it was time, and Randall went soon afterward. Ellen

stayed up to study; she hadn't finished her homework in the afternoon.

The following night Aunt Earnestine came to supper for the first time since her illness. Everyone made
a special effort to be nice to her, and Randall believed she was making an effort to be nice, too. Or
maybe she was still too weak to be bossy.

As soon as the meal was over she went back to her
room, but the following evening she stayed in the
kitchen longer.

"We'll play some games," said Ida, when the supper dishes had been cleared away.

"No, I don't think so," said Aunt Earnestine.

"Sure you will," said Ida. "I'm still the nurse and
in charge of the patient!"

Aunt Earnestine said, "There's no doubting you're
a good nurse." To everyone else she said, "If Ida
hadn't given me such splendid care, I honestly think
I'd have died."

Ida seemed embarrassed. "Find the cards, somebody," she said. "Are we gonna play a game, or aren't
we?"

There was a scramble to look for the playing cards,
and when the children and Ida were settled around
the table, Mr. Sutton pulled up a chair. "Better join
us," he coaxed Aunt Earnestine. "A little fun might
do you good."

Aunt Earnestine smiled. "Oh, well, I might join in for a hand or two of Old Maid."

Ellen dealt the cards, and the twins picked up each one of theirs as soon as it hit the table, chuckling as they peeked to see what they'd been given. Suddenly Dewey's smile disappeared, and he groaned, "Oh, no!"

Randall said, "That's practically telling everybody that you have the Old Maid."

"Right!" agreed Ida. "Expert cardplayers like us don't show any expression on their faces. It's called a poker face. See? Like this." She turned to the twins with a blank look. "Then nobody can guess whether you have good cards or bad ones."

"We'll try it," said Dewey, and he and Clay kept solemn faces as the game got under way.

Aunt Earnestine, who was on the other side of Dewey, drew a card from his hand, and he looked neither happy nor sad.

"That's it," said Ida. "You're getting onto it." But on the next round, when Aunt Earnestine drew a card, Dewey yelled, "Yippee!" and then laughed hysterically.

Aunt Earnestine turned to Mr. Sutton, on the other side of her, and held up her cards. "Go ahead, draw," she said a bit impatiently.

Mr. Sutton said, "If I draw the Old Maid, do you

promise not to yell, 'Yippee!' and burst out giggling?"

"I'm making no promises," said Aunt Earnestine, a faint smile crossing her face.

Randall laughed. He couldn't keep a poker face and think of Aunt Earnestine having a giggling spell.

Mr. Sutton had drawn the Old Maid from Aunt Earnestine before the game was over, Randall knew, because Randall himself, next around the table, drew the card from his father on his last play. He did not succeed in getting rid of it, and Clay and Dewey chanted happily, "Randall's the Old Maid! Randall's the Old Maid!"

While the cards were being shuffled for the next game, Mr. Sutton said, "Brother Preston came by the lumberyard this afternoon."

"Why hasn't he brought that donkey out here?" asked Ida. "Even a world-famous animal trainer like me needs time. Christmas'll be here before you know it."

"He's having trouble catching the donkey and wondered if some of you would lend a hand tomorrow. Randall, I told him you'd probably help him."

"We'll help!" said Dewey and Clay at the same time.

"Count me out," said Ellen. "I have a math test Friday and I have to study."

90

Clay said, "Ida'll help, won't you, Ida?"

Ida's eyes lit up. Then her expression became more solemn. "It'd be fun, but I'd better stay here and look after things."

Aunt Earnestine said, "Surely I'm able to do a bit around the house by now. Go with the boys if you want to. You need a change."

The idea of catching a donkey kept the twins in good spirits. They wouldn't have been happier, thought Randall, if they'd been invited to go to Africa to hunt lions and elephants. He waited with them and Ida at the gate to Mr. Talbot's pasture on Thursday afternoon. "It's a big pasture," he said, looking at one fenceline that disappeared over a hill. Another went into a swamp.

While everyone was trying to guess where the donkey might be, Brother Preston arrived, wearing brown corduroy pants and a red plaid sweater. He'd brought a halter and a piece of rope long enough for a lead. Randall suddenly remembered that Ida was an expert at using a lasso and wished he'd thought to bring a long rope along.

"Now the donkey may be in the swamp," said Brother Preston, "but let's check the rest of the pasture first." He led the way, and they walked for a long time—but no one sighted the donkey. Randall thought he saw it lying in a clump of bushes, but it turned out to be a big rock instead. They walked farther.

"Look!" said Dewey. "There it is!"

Sure enough, it was the donkey. It was coming out of the swamp into an open spot.

"Good!" said Brother Preston. "Now let's ease our way around to the other side of it." Randall expected the donkey to turn and run back into the swamp when it saw them, but it didn't. When they'd worked their way around it, Brother Preston said, "Now let's keep it between us and the fence. We'll fan out a bit and see if we can drive it toward that brier patch."

Slowly they made their way toward the donkey, who seemed as curious about them as they were about it.

"Now just take it easy," urged Brother Preston. Randall knew that he was saying it to the twins, who kept wanting to run ahead. They'd expected this to be a big chase, he knew, and they would be disappointed if the donkey let somebody just walk up and put a halter on it.

The donkey stood as still as a statue, and when they were almost up to it, Brother Preston whispered, "All right now, everybody stay where you are, and I'll catch it."

The donkey remained still, and soon Brother Preston stood directly in front of it. Less than an arm's length away, he raised the halter to slip it over the donkey's head. At that, the donkey jumped completely off the ground, turned around in the air, and kicked with both back legs. Brother Preston managed to jump out of the way but lost his balance and fell backward onto the ground. The donkey galloped off.

The twins laughed as if it were the funniest thing they'd ever seen.

After making certain that Brother Preston wasn't hurt, Ida asked him, "Is that the way you catch a donkey?"

She laughed, but Brother Preston didn't. He sprang to his feet. His face was red, and he looked angry.

Dewey reached out and patted his hand. "It was a joke," he said softly. At home, whenever the twins got mad at anyone who teased them, usually someone else would say, "It's a joke. Can't you take a joke?" Randall was glad Dewey hadn't added the last part of it.

The donkey had stopped near a stream, and

Brother Preston said, "Let's get it this time!" Again they made their way toward it slowly and quietly. When Brother Preston finally stood in front of it, the donkey whirled around again and kicked. Brother Preston leaped out of the way but did not fall. The donkey jumped the stream and sped away. The twins were delighted.

Partway up the hill, the donkey stopped and looked back. It appeared to be enjoying the chase almost as much as the twins were, thought Randall. Otherwise, it would run to the far end of the pasture—or make a break for the swamp.

Eventually they drove it into a corner. "We've got it this time!" said Brother Preston, making his way nearer.

"Be careful," warned Ida. "That barbed wire looks old and rusty. It might not hold if the donkey tried to bust through it. Besides, we don't want him scratched up."

Randall said, "He looks sort of moth-eaten to me. A scratch or two shouldn't hurt him."

"He's not moth-eaten," said Ida. "He just needs some brushing and looking after. Before you know it, he'll be the best-looking donkey that ever rode into Bethlehem."

Randall laughed, but Brother Preston said, "It's *not*

Bethlehem. The tableau is a *reproduction* of the scene that took place in Bethlehem."

"Well, anyway," said Ida, "he'll be the most handsome jackass there ever was!"

Clay said, "But he's a donkey."

"A jackass is a male donkey," explained Ida.

By then Brother Preston had walked up to the donkey and was patting it on the head. But when he tried to slip the halter over its ears, the donkey ran away. Brother Preston grabbed it by the neck but couldn't hold it back.

On the next try the donkey stood in the middle of an open space. Randall figured it would be impossible to catch it there. The donkey appeared to be waiting for them, and when they were almost to it, Dewey said, "I'll bet Ida could catch it."

"Yeah," said Clay. "Why don't you let Ida try it?"

"You two think Ida can do everything," said Brother Preston, sounding the least bit sarcastic.

Dewey said pleasantly, "Yes, that's what we think."

"Well, let's see her catch this donkey!" said Brother Preston. He handed Ida the rope and halter, and he stood with Randall and the twins while Ida made her way forward.

As Ida went nearer, she said soothingly, "Come on, friend, it's just ol' Ida wanting to take you to live with us for a while." The donkey looked at her. Randall wondered if it would flip around, kick at her, and take off. But it stood motionless. Ida patted it on the head. Then she rubbed its neck and ran her fingers along its mane. "You're needing a haircut," she said. "And how would you like some corn and hay when we get home?" She spoke soothingly. "How does that sound to you? It's poor pickings in a pasture at this time of year, wouldn't you say? Nothing much here but stubble."

The donkey looked at her as if it understood every word she said—and appreciated the sympathy. Randall half expected the donkey to say something back to her, but maybe this wasn't the time for that. Still, he'd bet that before Christmas was over it would have learned to talk.

Ida continued to speak in a gentle voice. When she stopped patting it, the donkey reached out its head to her. "Okay, if you insist," said Ida, but instead of patting it this time she slid the halter onto its head. "There! That's not so bad, is it?"

She started away, and the donkey followed her as if it would have come along whether it was on a lead or not.

"He was probably just tired of running around," said Ida.

"Yes," agreed Brother Preston. "That was it."

"You'd have caught him this time," she added.

Randall almost laughed. He knew that Ida was being careful not to gloat over having succeeded where Brother Preston had failed.

"See?" Dewey said. "There's not anything Ida can't do!"

The Checkers Tournament

Randall finished reading the twins their favorite story, *The Three Billygoats Gruff*, and Clay put the book back on the shelf beneath the window. He brought out another one, but Randall said, "Let's quit for a while." He'd been trying to keep Clay and Dewey quiet by reading to them.

"Then what can we do?" asked Clay. It was raining, and they couldn't play outside.

"We can talk if you'll keep your voices down." They'd made so much noise soon after they'd returned home from school that Aunt Earnestine had come into the kitchen and scolded them. She'd gone

98

back to her room now for the rest of her afternoon nap.

Randall felt sorry for the twins. Naturally, their spirits were high; it was a Friday afternoon—and close to holiday time, at that. Still, he could understand Aunt Earnestine's wanting them to quiet down. She was under the doctor's order to get lots of rest.

"Reckon Santa Claus will bring anything to Aunt Earnestine?" whispered Dewey.

"You don't have to whisper," said Randall. "She can't hear you in her room if you don't whoop and holler."

"I wouldn't bring her anything," said Clay. "If I were Santa Claus, I'd skip over Aunt Earnestine."

Ida Early and Ellen came into the kitchen. They'd been giving the front room—or parlor—its Christmas cleaning. The room was seldom used, except when company came—and not always then. Ida took the broom and tossed it across the kitchen. It landed in its place in the corner. "Your turn!" she said to Ellen, who was holding an old flour sack that was now a dustcloth.

Ellen whirled the cloth over her head and let it go. It sailed across the room, landing on a nail above the broom. "It's in the wrist movement!" she said, imitating Ida. They sat down with the boys.

"So what's going on back here?" asked Ida.

Randall said, "We're trying to decide if Santa Claus should bring a present to Aunt Earnestine."

"And should he?"

"Clay and Dewey think not."

"In that case," said Ida, "we must get busy and make a gift for her ourselves."

"Let's don't!" said Clay.

Ida pretended to be shocked. "Why, Clay, how terrible! You must remember: It is more blessed to give than to receive." She grinned and added, "That's in the Bible. At least, that's where I think it's from. We'll check with Brother Preston."

Brother Preston had continued to correct, sometimes scold, Ida and the children for any mistake they made in connection with the Bible. Mr. Sutton had said that probably he was just enthusiastic, from having recently been a student of it, and he wanted everyone else to become a Bible scholar, too.

"Let's go ride the donkey," said Dewey, hopping up from the table.

"Are you crazy?" asked Randall. "It's pouring down rain."

"We can ride in the rain." He looked at Ida. "Couldn't we ride in the rain?"

"Why, of course we could!" said Ida. "A little thing

like rain wouldn't hold us cowboys back. But on the other hand, the donkey needs to rest up for his starring role in the Christmas program."

Clay said, "But it's a long time till Christmas."

Ellen said, "Why, it's almost here! It's two weeks from Sunday."

Randall added, "Which means that two weeks from tomorrow is Christmas Eve."

"That's the day for the *tableau*," said Dewey. He and Clay had been learning to use the word.

"Right!" said Ida, patting him on the back. "And the day before that we practice for it." She and Randall were to be in the tableau. Randall was to be a shepherd, off to one side of the scene, but Mrs. Landis had insisted that Ida have a part that would put her alongside the manger, where she could handle the animals if they acted up. Brother Preston would not agree to adding a stablemaid to the cast, so Ida had volunteered to be one of the Wise Men. She'd said that with the robes she'd wear, and her height, nobody would know the difference. "I can either be a Wise Man," she'd said, "or the tallest Virgin Mary anybody ever saw!" Brother Preston had agreed then to her being a Wise Man.

"We want to go with you to practice for it," said Clay.

"I wouldn't consider going without you!" said Ida. "After all, you're my Assistant Animal Trainers. In fact, you're in complete charge of the turkey."

"And Frizzy," said Clay.

"Right. But Frizzy's so smart she's not going to need anybody to look after her. She'll perch on the end of the manger and be the best-behaved chicken there ever was! But the turkey might get restless and fly off. If he does, your job'll be to bring him back."

"To the *tableau*," said Clay.

"Exactly! You're in charge of the tableau turkey!"

"Look!" said Ellen, pointing toward the window. "The sun's out!"

"Now that it's stopped raining," said Dewey, "please, couldn't we ride the donkey? It can rest up later."

"Maybe the ol' boy would like a little company now that the sun's out," said Ida. "If Randall will lead him into the yard, I'll come out as soon as I help Ellen get supper started."

The twins ran from the house and were at the pasture gate when Randall got there. The donkey came from the barn to greet them—and to be petted through the fence. It didn't look like the same animal, thought Randall, they had brought here yesterday. It had had lots of corn and hay to eat and had been brushed till its coat was sleek. But it was still stubborn.

"Come on, ol' pal," said Randall, "let's see if you'll be friendly today." The donkey stretched its head forward, all but putting it into the halter himself. The twins laughed, and quickly they opened the pasture gate so Randall could lead the donkey into the back-yard.

As soon as they were on the path between the barn and the henhouse, the twins began begging to ride. Ida had let them ride partway home yesterday afternoon. "All right," said Randall, "but make sure you hang on."

He lifted Dewey onto the back of the donkey, and while he was reaching for Clay, the donkey bucked violently. Dewey was thrown high into the air and flipped over, as if he'd turned a somersault on purpose. He landed on his feet in the wet grass, appearing more surprised than anyone else that he was upright.

Randall cheered, and Clay said, "Do it again!"

"No," said Randall, "let's lead the donkey around till he's settled down."

In less than a minute Dewey said, "Okay, he's settled down. Let's try again."

This time the donkey waited till both Clay and

Dewey were on its back before it bucked. The twins held on for a few seconds and then fell off. There was nothing spectacular in their landing, but they hopped up and wanted to try once more.

By then Ida had come into the yard, and for the rest of the afternoon the donkey acted as if it had never once tried to throw anyone from its back.

After supper the family held a checkers tournament. Mr. Sutton and Randall were among the first losers, and they moved over and sat by the fire. The twins had lost, too, but they stayed on at the table.

Mr. Sutton pulled his big chair over to the hearth and poked at the coals. He'd been unusually quiet all evening, Randall thought. Maybe he was thinking about Christmases when Mrs. Sutton was living. Randall had been thinking about them, too. His mother had always enjoyed the holidays as much as the children.

Randall added a log to the fire and said, "It'll soon be time to cut a Christmas tree. I've picked out a small cedar that'll be just right."

"Yes," said his father. "We want to put up some decorations . . ." He poked at the fresh log and added, ". . . whether we're feeling merry or not."

"I came across a holly tree one day that's loaded down with berries. I'll go back and get some branches."

"Good," said Mr. Sutton.

"Maybe you could ask one of the lumberjacks to bring in some mistletoe," said Randall. Mistletoe usually grew so high up in trees that it was difficult to reach.

"Sure," said Mr. Sutton. "That's a good idea."

Randall thought of how his mother had always enjoyed decorating for the holidays. At this time of year she'd start putting together garlands of pine and cedar—with as many berries as she could find. Holly and mistletoe were her favorites. Although neither he nor Mr. Sutton said anything as they sat looking into the fire, Randall felt certain that his father was having the same thoughts that he was. Still, he hadn't meant to say aloud, "And while she was making the garlands—" He left off there, feeling a bit sheepish, as if he'd been caught talking to himself.

His father turned to him. "Yes," he said softly, "I remember. While she was making the garlands, she always hummed 'Jingle Bells.'" He reached over and clapped one hand on Randall's shoulder just as the twins booed loudly. Ellen had beaten Ida Early at checkers.

The twins came over to the fire and climbed into their father's lap, one on each side. Randall wished they'd stayed over at the table to watch Ellen and Aunt Earnestine in the final checkers match. But with Ida out of the tournament, they were more interested now in talking to their father about the donkey. After they'd told him about the rides—and the spills—of the afternoon, Clay said, "We're going to put on rodeo shows when we grow up!"

Mr. Sutton said, "But I thought you planned to run a circus."

Dewey said, "We'll have a circus *and* a rodeo." He and Clay argued about which one would be in charge of the circus and which one of the rodeo until Mr. Sutton reminded them that it was their bedtime.

"But the tournament's not over," said Clay.

"It's over now," said Ida, when Ellen had made a move with her last man that wiped out everything else on the board. "Ellen's the new champion!"

"That was fun," said Aunt Earnestine, getting up from the table. Then she looked at the children and asked, "If anyone besides Santa Claus were to give you a present at Christmas, what would you like it to be?"

"Anything," said Randall, but he knew that wasn't much of an answer if she really wanted ideas. "A shirt or a sweater would be nice," he added, knowing the suggestion should be for something practical. Aunt Earnestine always gave the children a gift at Christmas, even when she wasn't living with them, but it was always something they needed, never anything just for fun. One year she'd given them underwear.

Ellen said that she'd like bedroom slippers or a blouse. Aunt Earnestine turned to the twins. "What about you? What do you want?"

"The three billygoats gruff," said Dewey, and Clay said, "Yes, that's what we want!"

Aunt Earnestine smiled. "But you have that book. I've seen it on the shelf."

"No," said Clay. "We mean the *real* billygoats gruff."

Aunt Earnestine, starting toward her room, laughed and said, "I'll go to bed on that!"

The twins were mad that no one took their suggestion seriously. They were still complaining about it when Ida went with them to their room. Randall knew that she'd put them in a better humor with a funny song or a bedtime story.

Mr. Sutton folded the checkerboard and handed it to Ellen to put away. "I'm glad Earnestine joins us in our games," he said. "She needs to have some fun."

Randall had been thinking that his father was the one who needed to have some fun. He looked unhappy much of the time now, which wasn't like him. This was the first Christmas since Mrs. Sutton died, and, no doubt, he was sad. Also, he'd been worried about not having much money to spend for the holidays. At supper he'd told his children not to expect "a big Christmas" this year. The Depression was still not over.

Ellen said, "I'm glad Aunt Earnestine joins us in our games, too."

Randall said, "But not so glad that you didn't beat the socks off her!"

Ellen laughed. "Well, I can't help it if I'm a crackerjack checker player!"

Randall said, "You know, I'll bet you could beat those old men who sit around in back of the store at the crossroads playing checkers all the time."

"Maybe one day I'll challenge them," said Ellen. "Can't you just see them? I'd walk in and say, 'Okay, fellows, let me show you some real checker playing.' Of course, I'll have to learn to chew tobacco first, because that's the other thing they specialize in." Randall knew she was trying to get Mr. Sutton to smile. "They'll say, 'That scrawny little girl thinks she can play checkers.' Whereupon I'll spit tobacco juice across the store and then beat 'em, every one! That'd be a real accomplishment."

Mr. Sutton reached out and patted her on the shoulder. "It's a real accomplishment for you to help your Aunt Earnestine. Maybe at long last she's learning how to enjoy something. You know, she never had much childhood herself."

Ellen said, "Everybody has a childhood. At least, I never heard of anybody being grown before they've been a child."

"That's true, but what I meant is that Earnestine never had much fun when she was growing up. Childhood should be more carefree than it was for her. When our mother died, she wasn't more than ten or eleven—younger than either of you is now."

Randall and Ellen said nothing, and Mr. Sutton continued. "Dad was off trying to make a living for us most of the time, and Earnestine looked after Myrtle and me and ran the house when she should have been out playing herself." He was quiet for a moment and looked as if he might be remembering things that had happened so long ago that he'd almost forgotten them. Maybe some of the memories were painful, thought Randall, and he'd like to forget them. After another moment his father said, "I wonder what it would have been like if we'd had an Ida Early?"

Skipping Stones

Every fall Mrs. Todd entertained her Sunday school classes at her home. She lived on a farm just outside of town, and there was a big open field that was just right for playing games like "Capture the Flag" and "Red Rover." At the edge of the field there was a grove of hardwood trees—oaks, tulip poplars, and sweet gums, mainly—with a few pines scattered about, and on the other side of the grove a big pond.

"I'm sorry not to've been able to give you your party earlier," said Mrs. Todd. In other years it had been a wiener roast held in October or early November. "I'm wondering if maybe I've waited too late this year?"

"No, ma'am," said Jimmy Ryan. "You haven't waited too late."

"If you'd rather, we could hold off and have a picnic in the spring." No one said anything, and Mrs. Todd continued. "It's up to you. I only thought perhaps it's getting too near Christmas and everyone would be busy at other things. Or that maybe the weather's too nippy by now."

"No, ma'am," said Jimmy. "It's not too nippy." Randall had heard Jimmy say once that the only parties he'd ever been to were the ones Mrs. Todd gave.

Mrs. Todd smiled. "Then suppose we have our cookout this coming Saturday. Is that a good day?"

Everyone agreed that Saturday was a fine day, and that yes, they could be at Mrs. Todd's house by noon.

At the end of Sunday school Mrs. Todd told the Suttons, "Invite Ida to come along to our party. It would be especially nice to have her with us, and I'll invite our new minister, too."

Mrs. Casey, standing nearby, said, "They'd make a good couple, wouldn't they? Both of 'em being so tall and everything."

Mrs. Todd seemed embarrassed, "Well, I wasn't

trying to make a match. It's just that there are so few young single people in the community that I thought—"

"Never mind," said Mrs. Casey with a giggle. "There's nothing wrong in matchmaking." Randall liked Mrs. Casey but had always considered her a bit giddy. She turned to him now and said, "Tell Ida that *we* think down deep our new preacher's smitten with her."

After church the twins could hardly wait to get home and tell Ida about the wiener roast. "And you're invited!" said Dewey. "Mrs. Todd said she especially hoped you'd come."

"Yes," said Clay, "and Brother Preston'll be happy if you're there, too."

"Do you think so?" asked Ida, with a wink at Randall. "You don't suppose he's sweet on me, do you?"

"Yes," said Dewey, "we think he is."

Then Clay, sounding as serious as a character in Aunt Earnestine's soap opera, said, "Down deep Brother Preston loves you very much."

Ida shouted, "Hot-diggety-dog!" so loudly she could have been heard on the next mountain over.

Randall knew that her enthusiasm was for Clay's and Dewey's benefit, and he was not surprised that, when Saturday arrived, she said she wasn't going to the cookout. "No, I must stay here and look after Aunt Earnestine and the house."

Mr. Sutton, reading the paper over by the fire, said, "But I'll be here." He had come home at midmorning. "I'll need to run back to the lumberyard before dark for a minute, but you'll be home by then. Go along with the children. You'll have a good time."

"I think I'd better not."

Mr. Sutton added, "I'm sure Mrs. Todd would be grateful for the moral support."

"What's moral support?" asked Dewey.

"It means letting someone know that you stand back of them."

Clay asked, "Why does Mrs. Todd want somebody to stand in back of her?"

Mr. Sutton smiled. "Well, not really in back of her, but moral support is just a term for letting someone know you believe in what they're doing—without going to any real trouble yourself. However, Ida might be put to trouble. For instance, what if one of you fell into that big pond over at the Todds' place? Who'd jump in and fish you out?"

"Ida would!" chorused the twins.

"And if a wind came up at the wrong time and sparks from the wiener-roasting fire blew into the dry grass on that big field, who'd put out the fire?"

"Ida would!"

"In that case, I take it back. Ida would give much more than moral support. She'd be a real and genuine help to Mrs. Todd."

"All right," said Ida, "I'll go." And she and the children set off to the party.

The morning was cool but bright and sunny. "It's an absolutely glorious day!" said Ellen, whirling around a couple of times at the roadside while she and Randall waited for J.C. to come down the trail from his house. Ida and the twins had walked on ahead.

"I don't know who's the happiest," said Randall, "you or the twins."

Ellen said, "Pa almost made it sound too exciting, didn't he? Clay and Dewey'll be disappointed if nobody comes near drowning—or a brush fire doesn't break out."

"I know," said Randall. "And you'll be disappointed if Marcus is not there." Marcus Ragsdale was her special friend. The Ragsdales lived farther out in the county and were not in the church, but they were related to the Todds. Mrs. Todd always invited Marcus and his younger brothers to her Sunday school parties.

"Yes, I admit it," said Ellen, when J.C. was almost

to them. "I'll be sorry if Marcus isn't there."

This was the first time J.C. had been out since his illness, and Randall and Ellen, as they walked along, tried to fill him in on things that had happened at school while he'd been away. Soon they rounded a curve and came in sight of the Todds' farm. Marcus was waiting for them at the end of the driveway, and after a friendly welcome led them to the house and into his aunt's big living room.

When everyone had arrived, Mrs. Todd said, "All right. I believe we're all set." She waited till the boys and girls had buttoned up their sweaters and jackets, then said, "If somebody'll take this"—she pointed toward the biggest picnic hamper Randall had ever seen—"and if somebody else'll take this one"—she pointed to another,"and this . . . and this . . . we'll be off!"

Jimmy Ryan and Randall took the first hamper, one on each side, and Brother Preston and J.C. took the other. Ida, assisted by the twins, saw to it that a big bucket of hot chocolate got out to the field safely.

A fire was built in a clearing near the grove of trees, and the children ran in and out of the woods, bringing fallen branches and limbs and adding them to the fire. Then while the fire burned down to coals, a search got under way for sticks to use in roasting the wieners. They had to be just the right size. If one was too thick, it wouldn't pierce a wiener. If it was too thin, it would bend or break. By the time everyone had a stick, there were hot coals at the fire, and the wiener roasting got under way.

The older children helped the younger ones—first in roasting the hot dogs and then in dressing them. In addition to mustard and ketchup and onions, Mrs. Todd had provided sauerkraut and chili. Randall liked everything but the sauerkraut.

Soon everyone was seated around the campfire, laughing, talking, and eating—except Blake Gilmore, who'd dropped his hot dog onto the ground and had had to start over.

The children who'd been in Ida's Sunday school class the day she'd taught the lesson were especially happy that she was at the cookout. While they sat around the fire, Lisa Madison said, "When I told my mamma about the story you told us, she said she was glad to know I was paying attention in Sunday school." Ida laughed, and Lisa added, "And my daddy said he'd like to come next time and listen, too!"

Mrs. Todd said, "Well, tell your dad that he'd be most welcome."

Sue Croft said to Ida, "When I told my mamma

about the story you told us, she said that if you told another one, for me *not* to listen."

Ida laughed again, but Mrs. Todd frowned and said, "Well, dear, tell your mother that it would be nice if she'd help us sometimes with our classes." She'd emphasized "help us," which Randall knew meant she'd be glad if Mrs. Croft chose to do something besides criticize what others did. Of course, he knew there was no way to please everyone, and he wasn't really surprised that Ida's version of the "Loaves and Fishes" might have upset some parents. He smiled at Ida when he held out his cup, and she ladled a refill for him from the bucket of hot chocolate that rested in smoldering coals.

When the children had eaten all the hot dogs they wanted, Mrs. Todd opened big boxes of marshmallows. She said, "You may toast them or put them in your hot chocolate." She added, "Or do both!" as everyone scrambled to get to the marshmallows.

Randall took pride in being able to toast marshmallows till they were golden brown—just the way he liked them. If they were held over the coals one second too long, they would blaze up. Also, sometimes the inside of one would melt before the outside was toasted and the candy would slide off the stick into the fire. This happened twice to J.C. Jimmy Ryan and Ellen shared theirs with him.

"We can go down to the pond when everyone's finished eating," said Mrs. Todd, and the children began jumping up. "We're finished," they shouted, making a dash through the grove toward the pond.

"Now be careful!" called Mrs. Todd. "Wait for the rest of us."

Soon everyone was at the water's edge. "Can we go wading?" asked Jordie Williams.

Mrs. Todd said, "Oh, no, darling. You'd catch your death of cold. But do you know what my own children liked to do when they were growing up? They liked to skip stones."

This brought on a discussion of skipping stones. Some of the children had heard of it; some hadn't. Mrs. Todd explained that it was merely throwing stones in such a way that they skipped across the surface of the water.

"Yes, ma'am," said Jimmy Ryan. "Only we call it skimming stones."

Brother Preston said, "I've even heard it referred to as bouncing them. Here, I'll demonstrate." He picked up a small stone and threw it out across the pond, where it struck the surface of the water and bounced back into the air. The next time it hit the water it sank.

"I can do better than that," said Brother Preston, picking up another stone. "The best ones are thin and flat." He held up one that he considered good, then threw it. This one bounced, or skipped, four times before it sank.

Some of the boys and girls began trying to skip stones. Randall knew that it was not easy. Once in late summer he and Ellen and Ida, in a walk through the woods, had come to a series of beaver ponds, and Ida had taught him and Ellen how to skip stones. There was a knack to it, and Ellen had caught on to it immediately. She'd been much better at it than Randall, he had to admit. As for Ida—well, she had made stones all but dance across the water's surface that day. She'd made them skip, or bounce, as many as seven or eight times. She'd thrown one stone that had skipped between two tree stumps that were in the water, across a dam into another pond, over a beaver lodge, and into a knothole of a log that was floating there.

Brother Preston demonstrated the throwing technique again, once more succeeding in skipping a stone four times. Some of the boys and girls were having mild success, too. Marcus tried it but did not do well.

"You'll get better," said Ellen. "It takes a little

practice." Randall noticed that she didn't skip a stone herself. Maybe she was afraid she'd embarrass Marcus if she made it seem too easy.

Brother Preston handed Ida a stone. "Here," he said, "this one's just right. Try your hand with it."

The twins rushed over to watch. Although they hadn't been along at the beaver ponds, they knew that Ida was a whiz at throwing anything. Randall also thought that now she'd dazzle everyone with the best throw of the day. Instead, she threw the stone so clumsily that it didn't bounce even once. It went into the water with a dull *kerplunk*.

The twins looked as if they thought Ida was ill. Clay said, "Maybe it's in the wrist movement. Try again."

"No," said Ida. "I guess there are some things that other people can do lots better than I can."

Dewey said, "But not many, are there, Ida?" He and Clay might be promoting a romance, thought Randall, but at the same time they didn't want to admit that anyone could do anything better than Ida. "Cheer up," Randall whispered to them as they started away from the pond. "Love blooms forever!"

Reasons for Rehearsals

Mrs. Landis was in charge of the tableau, but it looked as if Brother Preston had taken over. "Tie the cow here," he said, touching a corner post on the manger, outdoors in front of the church, "and the donkey to the one down there."

While Ida and Randall tied the two animals to their places, Brother Preston told Mr. Ed Pickins, who was to be a Wise Man, where he was to stand. Everyone else milled about, chatting with one another. There were more people there than Randall had expected to see, but he'd forgotten that choir members were to be on hand, too. Mrs. Todd was in the choir; Randall waved to her. So was Mrs. Gilson, J.C.'s mother. J.C. stood off to the side, holding Archie, his two-year-old brother, in his arms. Jokingly, he'd offered to be the shepherd for Randall if Randall would keep up with Archie for him.

There were a few people standing around who were not on the program but had been passing by and had stopped to see what was happening. The church was only a block off Buckley's main shopping street, and naturally the Friday before Christmas was a big trading day.

"Let's see," said Brother Preston. "The chicken should go here," and Ida took Frizzy and placed her on the board at the foot of the manger.

"What about the turkey?" asked Clay. "Where do you want him?"

"The turkey is not to be in the tableau," said Brother Preston.

"But that's why he's here!" said Clay in a shocked tone. Dewey added, "He's been looking forward to it."

"Turkeys were not known in the Middle East when Christ was born," said Brother Preston, as if he were giving a lecture. "They're from the New World and therefore wouldn't have been in Bethlehem at that time."

Clay and Dewey may not have understood, but Brother Preston had said it with such authority that they didn't ask any more questions. They looked as hurt as if they'd been knocked down, thought Randall, and he tried to explain it to them when Brother Preston went to see about something else. "The New World is America," he said, "and it wasn't discovered till a long time after Jesus was born. And turkeys were here, I guess—if Brother Preston says so—and were not in Bethlehem."

"Neither was Frizzy," said Clay, patting the turkey, which was sitting in his lap. "Nor anybody else here."

Ida came over to help explain it. "Remember that story I told you once about Columbus discovering America?"

"Yes," said Dewey, "we remember it."

"Well, Columbus discovered turkeys, too. In fact, one of them was the very first thing he saw when he landed, and he told the crew with him, 'Ain't it too bad they didn't have a turkey in Bethlehem way back yonder? It sure would have cheered up Baby Jesus."

Brother Preston said, "You distort things, Ida." Randall hadn't realized he was within earshot.

"No, I just fill in a few of the details that somehow got left out."

Three women arrived then, bringing big boxes of costumes they'd made. Soon everyone who had a part in the tableau was trying on an outfit. The shepherds were to wear drab cloaks and tattered hats, and Mary and Joseph had rather ordinary garments too, but the robes for the three Wise Men—Mr. Pickins; Mrs. Todd's husband, Ralph; and Ida—were dazzling. Randall remembered that the Wise Men were sometimes spoken of as "the three kings." No doubt, it was fitting that their robes be items of splendor.

"The silver collar on this one," said one of the women, putting a robe on Mr. Pickins, "is from an evening dress I wore in a piano recital many years ago." The body of the robe was a rich blue, and the big sleeves were red-and-white striped, which reminded Randall of the lounging pajamas that brightened up the window of the dry goods store— the pair Ida had talked about.

The second lady, brushing down the collar of the robe she'd put on Mr. Todd, said, "This one's from my going-away dress when I got married."

Mrs. Landis said, "Better than patchwork quilts! When I was little, I loved the quilts my mother made because I could recognize bits in them of clothes I'd outgrown."

The third robe was unfolded It was as colorful as

the first two, but when it was tried on Ida, it was much too short.

Mrs. Landis winked at Randall. "That's why we have rehearsals."

Ida said, "I could kneel down, and it wouldn't be noticeable."

"Why, no, indeed!" said the woman who was helping her with the costume. "It'll be no trouble to add a strip of something splendid." She called across the yard, "How about it, Ruthie? Anything left of your recital dress?"

Brother Preston turned to the couple who were to be Mary and Joseph and began showing them where they were to stand. When they'd taken their places, the donkey kicked at Joseph, barely missing him. Brother Preston was having them move a safer distance away when someone said, "Here come the sheep!"

Abner Haywood, a classmate of Ellen's, was driving them across the parking lot. At a distance, it looked as if there were three sheep, but one of them was Abner's big, shaggy dog. When they had almost reached the manger, Brother Preston said, "Just stay where you are till I finish here."

Mrs. Landis went over and greeted Abner warmly. "I'm so glad you've made it," she said. "Somehow when I picture the Christmas scene, the shepherds and their flocks are the first things that come into my mind."

A lady from the costume committee brought Abner his shepherd's staff and the cloak and tattered hat that he was to wear. Mrs. Landis said to Randall, "Why don't you stand near Abner?"

"That's all right," said Brother Preston, turning to Abner and Randall, "but you need to be farther back." He was looking at them, deciding on the distance they should be from the manger, and hardly glanced at the sheep. "Move back a bit more, please." The boys stepped backward, but the sheep, with the dog between them, remained where they'd been. "Come on!" said Brother Preston impatiently. "Back up." He reached down as if he were shooing the animals. The dog growled—and then snapped at Brother Preston's leg.

Brother Preston jumped back. "That's not a sheep!" he shouted.

"Who said it was?" asked Abner.

"It's a dog!" said Brother Preston.

"Yes, I know."

"Well, what's it doing in the tableau?"

"Protecting the sheep."

Mrs. Landis came back over to them. "Maybe Clay

and Dewey could persuade the dog to come over to the sidelines with them." She asked Abner, "Do you think that might be all right?"

"Yes, ma'am, it'd be fine." He called to the twins, "Just whistle for him—he'll come. His name's Buster."

Clay and Dewey couldn't whistle, but they called, "Here, Buster! Come over here!" and the dog ran to them. The turkey, evidently thinking it was being attacked, flew out across the manger and into a tree out near the street. It lit on a low branch and from it flew onto another one and then another till it was at the top of the tree.

"Oh, dear!" said Mrs. Landis. "Now what'll we do?"

"Don't worry," said Ida. "It just wants a better view of everything that's going on down here. It'll come back when we're ready to go home."

Brother Preston looked annoyed, and Mrs. Landis said soothingly, "That's why we have rehearsals. But don't despair—the turkey won't be here for the real performances." She turned to Abner and said, "Maybe Buster won't be here, either—what do you think?"

"I reckon I could leave him at home," said Abner.

"All right, choir members," Brother Preston said. "If all of you will stand over here, we'll go to work on the music."

Mrs. Landis said, "But there's no need for anyone else to have to stay, is there?"

Brother Preston thought a moment. "No, I suppose not."

Mrs. Landis said, "All of you know your places now. The costumes will be exactly right by tomorrow, so just get here in time to put them on. And I must say that all of you are perfect for the parts you're to play. It's going to be a marvelous program, I'm sure. Now get home safely with all your animals, and we'll see you tomorrow afternoon."

Randall put Frizzy in her traveling cage, the wire box that Ida had made for her, and then began unhitching the cow and the donkey from the manger. Ida, followed by the twins, went nearer the big tree out by the street. Ida held out one arm and made a gobbling sound. The turkey flew from its perch directly onto her outstretched arm. The members of the choir cheered, and Ida grinned at them.

On the way home the twins took turns carrying the turkey in their arms. They still were upset that it was not to be in the tableau. The turkey, however, was happy enough; it pecked contentedly at a button on Dewey's shirt.

Ida tried to cheer up Clay and Dewey. "Aren't you proud of Frizzy?" she said excitedly, as if sitting on the end of the manger, doing nothing, had required great talent. "I'd certainly have hated it if *she'd* been left out of the program. Why, she has a real knack for show business!"

The Afternoon Performance

The choir sang two carols—very poorly. Anyone
might have thought they hadn't practiced, but Randall knew they had. Besides, carols were so familiar
that almost anyone who could sing at all knew them.
And there were some really fine voices among the
choir members; visitors to the church had often re-
marked on it. So the only way Randall could account
for their weak performance now was that they were
nervous in facing the large audience. He'd never seen
such a big crowd anywhere. It looked as if all the
people who'd been in town for last-minute Christmas
shopping had stopped long enough to stand in front

of the church and watch the program. The crowd spilled over into the parking lot and the road out front.

Everyone was invited to join in singing the next song, which was "Silent Night." At the end of the first verse, a high, loud, and squeaky voice sang out, "Yodle-li-de-lady, Yodle-li-de-lady."

Everyone looked at Frizzy. It sounded for all the world as if the hen had done the yodeling. Frizzy, of course, was perched at the foot of the manger, doing nothing more special than blinking her eyes every now and then. While heads were turned toward her, the finishing touch to the yodel began, sounding as if it were coming from the other end of the manger. The crowd looked at the donkey, which was moving his lips, trying to reach the hay at the head of the doll that represented the newborn babe. But it looked—and sounded—as if it were the donkey which added in a hoarse, deep voice, "Yodle-li-de-lady-oh!"

Almost everyone in the audience laughed. Only Brother Preston looked annoyed. Members of the choir smiled and appeared more relaxed now, and on the rest of their songs they did a marvelous job. The audience seemed almost spellbound then—listening to good voices singing out favorite Christmas songs while looking at the reproduction of the scene

131

at Bethlehem. Of course, when they were asked to join in singing another song, Randall suspected that most of them hoped there'd be yodeling again. But Brother Preston, he knew, had guessed right off where the sounds had really come from; he glared at Ida at the end of each verse as if he dared her to add even one extra note. There was no more yodeling.

At the end of the song service the audience was invited to walk around the manger scene for a closer look, but everyone was hesitant about going near. When no one walked over to the manger, Ida, keeping her place with the other two Wise Men, said, "Step right up, folks! Move in close now! Come right up!"

Randall would bet this was the first time a Wise Man had ever invited an audience to step in closer, but there was no doubting that the invitation was effective. People began to go nearer, and soon they were circling the manger. Ida continued. "Come right along, folks! See the Christ Child lying in the manger. And don't be afraid to smile. Christmas is a happy time! We're here to celebrate the birthday of the Lord!"

"Right!" sang out a frail-looking old lady Randall had noticed earlier. He had wondered how she'd had strength to be out on a chilly afternoon by herself. "Joy to the world!" she added in an even stronger voice.

It was as if the words were a match struck to set the song ablaze, because everyone burst into singing the carol. "Joy to the world, the Lord is come," it began. It had not been sung in the service earlier.

But it's sure being sung now! thought Randall. It sounded as if people for miles around were lifting their voices this time. But he knew this was because the voices were being magnified by echoes from the surrounding mountains.

When the song ended, people began to leave. They called "Merry Christmas," to each other and to the characters in the tableau, who still held their places. When the last visitor had gone, everyone was dismissed until the evening program.

Ida handed her robe to Randall to turn in while she took the cow and donkey across the road. A family who lived there had an old wagon shed in their backyard. They'd offered to look after the animals for anyone who wanted to leave them in town till the second program. Abner drove his sheep over there, too.

Frizzy was no trouble to carry around, so she was to be taken home and brought back later. Randall put her in the cage and returned the costumes to Mrs. Landis and the ladies who'd made them.

"Wasn't it moving?" asked Mrs. Landis as she helped fold costumes.

"Yes, it was," said Randall.

By then Ida was back, and she and Randall went across the yard to join Ellen and the twins for the walk home. Just as they were starting away, Brother Preston caught up with them. Randall was sure there'd be a short sermon preached then and there on how religion was a very serious matter. Instead, Brother Preston told Ida, "It won't be necessary for you to come to the evening performance."

Ida shrugged. "Oh, I don't mind coming back."

"I'll find someone else to take your place."

"You needn't bother. I'll be here." Ida looked slightly worried now.

"That was *too much*!" said Brother Preston. "The donkey and the chicken yodeling!"

Ida laughed. "We just got warmed up this afternoon. You wait till tonight!"

"And telling people to step right up! You sounded like a barker for a sideshow!"

"Maybe I did," said Ida. "But wasn't it wonderful how folks acted then? They began to really enjoy themselves and the tableau." She smiled as she added,

"And they suddenly caught the Christmas spirit when that little old lady shouted, 'Joy to the world!' "

"We are *not* Holy Rollers," said Brother Preston. "Our church is one of dignity."

Ellen spoke up. "But that woman was dignified. She was moved, but she was dignified and joyous at the same time. And everybody else was somehow moved—the spirit spread!" Randall was surprised. Evidently Ellen was still moved, because she rushed on. "And, anyway, some of the people there may have been Holy Rollers. Only a few people were from our church. Most of them were in town shopping and came over to have a look. One of my classmates from school who's Jewish was there to hear the music, and she told me afterward that she'd loved it. There were a lot of different people with a lot of different kinds of religion there—maybe some with no religion at all. And I think they all felt a warmer welcome to our service because of that old lady—and Ida!"

Brother Preston must have been as surprised as Randall, because he said nothing for a moment. Ellen was trembling. Randall suspected that the outburst had taken her by surprise, too.

Ida, grinning at Brother Preston, said, "So I'll see you tonight."

He did not smile back. "I'm trying to tell you—I don't want you in the tableau tonight. Can't you understand? I was trying to tell you in a nice way, but you won't listen to anything you don't want to hear. I'll say it again." Emphasizing each word, he said slowly and firmly, *"You are not to be in the tableau tonight!"*

Ida looked stunned. There was no doubting that she'd heard him this time.

Randall was embarrassed. Also, he was mad. He remembered that once—it seemed a long time ago to him now—friends of his had taunted Ida, and he hadn't come to her aid. He'd sworn then that he'd never again fail to be loyal to someone he cared about. Before he realized what he was saying, he shouted at Brother Preston, "Ida is our true friend!"

He was afraid that his shouting had scared the twins. They each grabbed one of Ellen's hands. Ellen, however, had regained her composure. "Should we take the donkey and the cow home?" she asked.

"No," said Brother Preston. He seemed shocked that she would ask such a question.

"Who'll handle them?" asked Ellen.

"I will, or Randall will, or somebody will. No, we need them. Everything else will be the same."

"I see." To everyone else, Ellen said, "Then come

along. Let's go home." It was almost as if she were the mother of them all and Ida were one of her children.

Ida didn't move. She stood there as if she were in a daze. Randall reached out and took one of her hands. "Come on," he said.

"Oh, yes, that's right," said Ida, shaking her head. "We'd better go, hadn't we?" As they started away, she turned and called back, "Merry Christmas, Brother Preston!"

Christmas Eve Night

The twins wanted to go to the program after supper, but Mr. Sutton wanted them to stay home. "You'll have more fun tomorrow if you rest tonight."

Aunt Earnestine said, "You look tired yourself. Maybe you'd better stay home, too."

"No, it shouldn't be very strenuous to listen to Christmas carols."

"Then we'll go, too," said Clay.

His father patted him on the shoulder. "No, we'll let you stay home. Go to bed on time, okay? And when you wake up in the morning, maybe Santa Claus will have been here."

Aunt Earnestine had decided that the night air would not be good for her, so she stayed home, too. She and the twins were playing five-card draw, a poker game that Ida had taught them, when Ellen, Randall, and Mr. Sutton got ready to leave for the program. Ida was washing the supper dishes.

Ellen said, "I should stay here and help you."

"Me, too," said Randall.

"No," said Ida, smiling at them. "I know you're my true friends. Go on and enjoy Christmas Eve. It's a special night, no matter where you spend it."

At the church Mr. Sutton drove into the parking lot. "Not a very good turnout," he said when he saw how few cars were there. "But we're early. Still, I'd imagine 'most everybody came this afternoon."

Randall hurried across the road to the wagon shed to bring out the donkey and cow. Quickly he put a halter on both of them and started away. The cow came willingly, but the donkey would not budge. Randall pulled, but the donkey still wouldn't move. Then he got behind it—and slightly off to the side, since he didn't want to be kicked—and pushed. The donkey still wouldn't move. Abner arrived to fetch the sheep, and he gave Randall a hand at pulling and tugging and pushing—even slapping the donkey on the flank. Still the donkey would not move.

139

Just then Buster, Abner's dog, came running into the shed as if he'd been called. "Oh, no!" groaned Abner. "You were supposed to stay home. I'm a good mind to whip you for following me." The way he patted Buster at the same time, Randall doubted he'd ever seriously considered whipping him. Abner continued. "Come on now. You ain't gonna like it, but I'm gonna lock you in this harness room over here."

"Will he stay?" asked Randall.

"No, he'll climb out. But it'll hold him till the program gets under way. Besides, he ain't gonna do any harm if he shows up. He knows how to behave."

They tried again to coax the donkey into moving, but it still wouldn't budge. Finally Randall led the cow across the road and tied her to the manger.

"The donkey won't come," he said to Brother Preston.

"It's got to!"

"I know. But I couldn't make it move."

"I'll go help you," said Brother Preston. As they started across the road, Randall motioned to his father, and he came to help them, too.

But as strong—and as determined—as they were, the three of them together could not budge the donkey. After exhausting themselves, Mr. Sutton said, "There's nothing else we can do. We sure can't lift it across the road."

"But we must have it!" said Brother Preston. "It was a donkey that Joseph led into Bethlehem with Mary on its back the night Christ was born."

Randall said, "Ida could get it to move."

Brother Preston bristled, but after a few seconds he said, "Yes, I suppose you're right."

Mr. Sutton said, "I'll go back home and get her. Start the program on time, and we'll have the donkey in place as soon as we can—*if* we can."

Randall hurried to pick up his costume, and soon he was in his place in the tableau near Abner and the sheep. He thought it would serve Brother Preston right if Ida refused to help, but he was ashamed of himself for having such a thought. He noticed that Mr. Alvin Jordan, one of the tallest men in the church, had become the third Wise Man for tonight. Randall didn't think he looked quite right for the part, but maybe that was because the robe was too long for him.

The choir started singing, and the program was under way. The donkey was still not there. Randall supposed that Ida had chosen not to be of help. He couldn't say he blamed her.

Partway through the second song, he heard the clip-clopping sound of the donkey crossing the road, and a moment later Ida was tying it to the manger Then she ducked into the shadows, off to the side and out of the bright lights that were focused onto the tableau. A short distance from her he saw Buster. Randall expected him to run to Abner, but instead Buster stood quietly as if he'd come to enjoy the program.

When the audience joined in singing "Silent Night," Randall half expected to hear yodeling at the end of each verse. But there was none. He was sure that Brother Preston would be pleased. Then he noticed that Mary and Joseph, in back of the donkey, were standing closer to it than they should have been. He hoped it wouldn't kick one of them. But the donkey stood perfectly still.

The only animal that moved at all was one of the sheep. To keep the sheep in their places, they'd tethered them by a short length of twine to a peg that had been driven into the ground. One of the sheep, in straining to reach a bit of grass stubble, had broken the twine and was moving on to another clump of grass.

Randall nudged Abner and pointed to the sheep. "Don't worry," whispered Abner. "It won't try to get past the crowd." The audience formed a circle around the entire scene.

The sheep went a bit farther . . . and a bit farther . . . and people near it backed away, giving it more room to graze. Then suddenly Buster, Abner's big, shaggy dog, raced into the crowd, barking loudly.

Someone screamed, "Mad dog!" and there were shrieks and screams from all sides.

Abner jumped up and yelled, "No! No! He's not mad! He's just trying to round up a stray sheep. He's *my* dog!" Randall hadn't known anyone could yell so loudly, but Abner had been heard over all the other noise. Members of the audience began to settle down, but not before some of them had backed farther away, leaving a gap in the circle.

The sheep dashed through the gap out into the night, with the dog, Buster, in pursuit. Abner and Randall chased after them, and a short way across the churchyard they saw why Buster had not wanted the sheep to wander. A big yellow dog lurked nearby. Randall had seen it occasionally on the streets in town; it was nobody's pet and it lived by scavenging. His father, in warning the family to stay away from the dog, had once described it as "tough, mean, and hungry."

The yellow dog sprang now at the sheep, grabbing it by the throat. Buster leaped onto the yellow dog. The three animals rolled over and over in the corner of the church parking lot.

"Stand back!" shouted Brother Preston as he raced

up to them. "Dog fights can be dangerous!" Taking Randall's shepherd's staff—a long cane with a crook for a handle—he started trying to break up the fight. Abner took his shepherd's staff and tried to hit the yellow dog. But every time he swung, the sprawling animals would tumble over, and he'd swat Buster or the sheep instead.

Suddenly Ida appeared. "Here," she said, "let me try it." Abner gave her his shepherd's staff. Instead of hitting at the animals with it, she held onto the straight end and, with the crook at the opposite end, managed in a flash to hook the yellow dog around the neck and snatch him out of the fracas. Before the dog knew what had happened, Ida grabbed it by the nape of the neck and threw it partway across the road. Randall thought, Maybe she *did* sling a dragon into a lake! The yellow dog looked back and snarled, but when Ida stamped her feet, it turned and ran away.

Quickly Ida examined Buster and the sheep. "Only small nicks," she said of the wounds. "Put pine tar on them when you get home, Abner, and they'll be fine. But hurry now! Back to the tableau!"

Soon Abner, Randall, the sheep, and Buster were in place near the manger. Brother Preston made an announcement. "Thanks to quick action by the shepherds—and a friend—the untimely situation has been put down. Our program will continue." Ida grinned at Randall and stepped back into the shadows.

The sheep that had not broken its tether lay down on the ground, and soon the other one and Buster lay down also. Randall imagined they were worn out from the excitement. He was glad they were still.

Now it was Frizzy who was fidgety. She hopped into the hay in the manger and then back onto her perch at the end of it. No sooner would she appear settled there than she'd hop back into the hay. At last she stayed in the hay in one little spot, and Randall was glad. He'd have hated for her to have flown suddenly out into the crowd. Probably the bright lights confused her; she wasn't used to staying awake after dark. But she sat still now; he supposed she was taking a nap. Then suddenly, just as the choir was singing softly "It Came Upon a Midnight Clear," Frizzy began to cackle.

Randall almost laughed; he was certain it was Ida adding a lively touch. Good for her! But Frizzy was cackling so loudly and went on for so long that he doubted that Ida would be doing it. The cackling was drowning out the choir. Then Frizzy hopped onto her perch at the end of the manger, still cackling. Randall had never known her to behave in such a way. Then he saw it: she had hollowed out a little nest in the hay at Baby Jesus's feet and had laid an egg!

Finally Frizzy quieted down. Instead of sitting on her perch, she stood on it and craned her neck toward the egg as if it were the most marvelous thing in the world. No doubt it was to her, thought Randall. Something to cackle about, for sure.

At the end of the service everyone was invited, as in the afternoon, to have a closer look at the figures in the tableau. Perhaps because it was a smaller crowd this time, made up for the most part of members of the church who knew each other, they did not need coaxing to walk up to the manger. Almost everyone smiled on seeing the egg, and when Mr. Sutton saw it he laughed out loud.

That alone was a good Christmas present, thought Randall. If Frizzy's laying an egg could make his father less sad, then hooray for Frizzy!

Randall looked around for Ida; he wanted to make certain that she saw the egg, but she wasn't in the shadows. He looked everywhere, but she was nowhere to be seen.

Christmas Morning

Clay and Dewey were in the kitchen, playing, when the rest of the household began to wake up. Of the toys Santa Claus had left under the tree for them, their favorite was a tiny boat, less than two inches long. It was powered by a candle no bigger than an acorn that sent it chugging out across the dishpan of water that was their boat basin. They also liked the toy tractor, fire engine, and marbles that had been left for them.

Santa had left Randall and Ellen a gift together—a game of Monopoly. "And you said we'd never have a set of our own," said Ellen.

"I said we'd never be able to *buy* a set of our own." Randall opened the board on the big table and began to spread out the various pieces that had come with it. Ellen joined him after she'd gone over and hugged her father, who was helping the twins relight the candle in their boat.

"Let's start a game right now," said Ellen.

"Before breakfast?" asked Randall.

"Well, just a little practice session then," said Ellen, rolling the dice. "We'll clear it away when we set the table." She laughed when the dice came up with a pair of sixes. "But after we eat, we'll spread it back out and play Monopoly *forever!*"

Randall was happy about the game, too, and he called to his father, "When you've finished over there, come see *our* present!"

Also, Randall and Ellen each had a gift from Aunt Earnestine—a warm zip-up jacket for Randall and a bathrobe and bedroom slippers for Ellen.

There were fruit and nuts in the stockings that had been hung on the mantelpiece. The Suttons grew their own pecans and apples, but at Christmas it was fun to have exotic things like English walnuts, Brazil nuts, and tangerines. Other years there'd been a few firecrackers and sparklers in the stockings, too, but there were none this time. Merchants in town hadn't been allowed to sell fireworks this year because some people considered them dangerous. Randall was sorry; lots of things could be dangerous, he knew, if not used with care. Fireworks were legal in the next town, but maybe Santa Claus hadn't been able to get there.

Santa had left Aunt Earnestine a small basket filled with dried flowers from the woods and fields. Randall had seen Ida weaving the basket.

The twins were so busy playing with their toys that they didn't pay attention to anyone else till suddenly Dewey asked "Where's Ida?" He sounded alarmed.

Nobody answered at first. Then Ellen looked up from the Monopoly board and said, "She's gone."

"Gone where?"

"We don't know."

Mr. Sutton said, "My guess is that she wanted to be by herself for a while. Maybe she wanted to think about Christmases when she was a little girl. We all need time to be alone occasionally."

"But she wouldn't leave without anybody here to look after us!" said Clay.

"No, she wouldn't," said Dewey, not sounding as sure of it as Clay. "Would she?"

"She didn't exactly leave you stranded," said Mr. Sutton. "I'm here, Randall and Ellen are here, you have each other, and there's Aunt Earnestine."

"We'd rather have Ida," said Clay.

Mr. Sutton laughed. "But you have us instead! And who knows but what somebody'll scare up some breakfast around here for all of us."

"I'll get it started," said Aunt Earnestine. Ellen and Randall helped her, and after a while everyone was seated at the table.

"I don't like scrambled eggs," said Clay, when the platter of sausage and eggs was being passed around. Ida had always fried an egg for him.

"I thought we'd have pancakes," said Dewey. "Ida made pancakes on special occasions. I thought Christmas was a special occasion."

"We're doing the best we can," said Ellen. "Next time you can fix breakfast."

When the meal was almost over, there was a loud, popping noise outside.

Aunt Earnestine jumped. "What on earth?" she said, spilling milk that she'd intended for her coffee onto the table.

Randall hurried to the window. "It sounded like firecrackers."

"Oh, boy!" said the twins.

"No," said Aunt Earnestine, "it sounded like gunfire!"

"Maybe it's rabbit hunters," said Mr. Sutton. "But they shouldn't be near the house. I'll go out in a minute and chase them off."

Just then there was another round of popping sounds. This time it was even closer, and Randall opened the back door. "Somebody's in the yard," he said.

Everyone hopped up from the table and ran onto the porch. When all the family was outside, a string of firecrackers was thrown onto the ground from behind the well. It was a long pack of small ones; Randall knew the kind. Their fuses were plaited together in such a way that when the main fuse was lighted, the spark from it reached one cracker at a time, setting it off just ahead of the next. They exploded rapidly, like machine-gun fire, and the pack danced across the yard.

The twins, on the porch, danced about, too— jumping up and down, squealing merrily. When the noise died down, Ellen teased them. "We're being attacked!" Then she called loudly, "We surrender! Come on out!"

Ida stepped from behind the well, where she'd been crouching. Randall was certain that by then everyone but the twins had guessed who was there. Of course, they wouldn't have been happier if it had been Santa Claus himself. Neither, he had to admit, would he.

"I was afraid all of you would be asleep and might need some waking-up," said Ida as she set off another loud batch of the firecrackers.

"Do some more!" said Clay when there was quiet again.

"That's all the noisemakers I have. I had one more string of 'em, but I set it off in the preacher's yard when I came past!"

The twins laughed, and Randall asked, "Did you wake up Brother Preston?"

"Yeah, he stumbled onto the porch, asking if I didn't know that this was Christmas. I told him that of course I did, and because it's Christmas I was making a joyful noise! Then I asked him to come out and eat supper with us tonight." She looked across the yard at the turkey, who was peeking around the corner of the smokehouse. "You can come out now," she called. "The shooting's over for a while!" As if he'd understood, the turkey strolled into the yard— followed by Frizzy, who was followed by the red rooster, two guineas, and the duck.

"What's in the bag?" asked Clay, looking at the paper sack at Ida's feet.

"All sorts of pretties," said Ida, picking up the bag.

"Fireworks that are even better than the crackers—Roman candles and skyrockets and sparklers. We'll have us a time tonight!"

Aunt Earnestine asked, "Is Brother Preston going to join us?"

"Yes, he said he would. He and I may not agree on everything, but at least we can talk about it." With a chuckle she added, "And he likes my cooking."

Everyone moved back into the kitchen, and Mr. Sutton said, "How about some breakfast? We're just winding up."

"No, thanks. I ate at a little roadside place across the mountains where I went to get the fireworks." She sat down at her usual place and pushed the plate aside but accepted the cup of coffee that Ellen brought her. Then while Aunt Earnestine cleared the table and Ellen and Randall washed dishes, Ida drank her coffee and told about hiking across the mountains. "Everything was so still," she said, "and the moonlight somehow seemed different from other nights. It's hard to explain, but when I stood on High Mountain and looked out over the countryside, I kept thinking, this is it: 'Silent night, holy night; all is calm, all is bright.' " Ida looked almost embarrassed to be talking like this, but she continued. "I stopped at the same spot on my way back, and the sun was coming up. There'd been a heavy frost, and in the first light of day everything glistened as if it had been dipped in silver. For me, the splendor of the greatest cathedral in the world couldn't compare with it."

"Did any bears get after you?" asked Clay.

Ida laughed. "No, but I got after some bears! I caught a big one by the tail and was bringing it home to you, but I had to turn it loose when a wildcat and a mountain leopard jumped on me at the same time."

While Ida and the twins talked about wild animals, the work was finished in the kitchen. Aunt Earnestine went back to her room, and the twins went back to playing with their new toys.

Half an hour later Ellen and Randall were teaching Mr. Sutton and Ida how to play Monopoly when there was a knock at the door. Randall opened it, and a tall man in overalls asked, "Is this where the lady lives who answered my ad in the *Market Bulletin*?" The *Market Bulletin* was a publication of Georgia's Department of Agriculture. It listed things that people wanted to sell or buy.

Ida said, "It wasn't me."

"Not me," said Ellen.

Mr. Sutton was telling the man that he might try the next house down the road when Aunt Earnestine came into the room. "Oh, yes," she said when she heard what they were talking about. "I wrote to you. Did you get my check? I sent it with the letter."

"Yes, ma'am," he said. "Everything's fine." Aunt Earnestine went onto the porch and closed the door. A moment later she opened it, and the man brought a big box inside and put it in the middle of the floor. He thanked Aunt Earnestine and left.

"It's for Clay and Dewey," said Aunt Earnestine. "Someone told me that *everybody* doesn't like clothes as Christmas presents."

The twins dashed for the box and lifted the lid Inside was the smallest goat Randall had ever seen. It was black-and-white and looked as much like a toy as a real one. Then it bleated; it was real, all right. The twins patted it lovingly, and it seemed pleased by their attention.

Aunt Earnestine said, "When it grows up it'll give milk, which I understand is quite nourishing."

Randall thought, She has to see a practical use for everything. Still, he was proud of her.

Mr. Sutton said, "Goat's milk makes good cheese, I'm told. But, Earnestine, aren't you always saying we have too many animals around here?"

"You do! But I'll be going home soon, and if you want a menagerie, that's your business." She turned to Ida and said, "There's a gift for you on your bed '

"Another goat?" asked Clay, and everyone laughed as Ida left the room.

A moment later Ida shouted, "Hot-diggety-dog!" so loudly that the goat was frightened. It leaped from the box.

"Look how high that fellow can jump!" said Mr. Sutton.

Clay said, "If it's gonna give milk, it's not a fellow," and Mr. Sutton laughed.

Dewey ran to pick up the goat, but it made another leap, this time across the arms of a rocking chair.

"Let's all be still a minute," said Mr. Sutton, "and give it a chance to settle down." The goat looked around, and when no one made a move toward it, it no longer seemed frightened. It walked over to Aunt Earnestine's feet, stretched out its neck, and began to nibble at the dried flowers in her Christmas gift.

"Stop it," she said, snatching the basket away.

At that, the goat leaped across a stack of firewood on the hearth and onto the rug beneath the Christmas tree. Mr. Sutton made a lunge for it, but he lost his balance. Instead of catching the goat, he turned the Christmas tree over onto Clay and Dewey. They scampered out and tried again to catch the goat.

After a neat, high jump across the footstool near

Mr. Sutton's big chair, the goat landed in the box in which it had arrived. Quickly Randall shut the lid. "Captured!" he said, just as Ida burst into the room.

She was wearing lounging pajamas—the red-and-white-striped ones that had been in the window of the dry goods store. She'd brushed her hair back and looked radiant. "I've never had such a grand present!" she said, walking out across the kitchen. She turned first one way and then another, showing off her new outfit. "Ain't I a splendid sight?"

Dewey said in his soft voice, "Don't forget, Ida, it's more blessed to give than to receive."

"That's right!" said Ida, lifting him into the air and swinging him around. "But there are times when receiving is pretty good, too!"

About the Author

Robert Burch, the author of *Queenie Peavy* and other popular books, was born in Fayette County, Georgia, and grew up there with seven brothers and sisters. Despite the economic hardships of the 1930s, he relishes many happy memories of those years. "We got by without store-bought toys, and we invented our own games. Pets were farm animals—a calf, a rooster, a turkey, or a pig." After years of traveling Mr. Burch has returned to rural Georgia. He now lives in a house only two miles from the one in which he grew up.

Robert Burch says, "A new story of Ida Early and the Sutton family is under way. When I'm not at work on it, I'm usually outdoors. There's a small pond in the backyard, and I'm having fun raising fish—goldfish and Japanese carp (or *koi,* as they are called), which are like *very big* goldfish. Some of mine are two feet long. And I have two dogs—my first ever. Their names are Willy and Omar, and they're good company. Omar is sweet but very average, while Willy is so smart that I may teach him to read and write!"